THE BUS

THE BUS

*Cosmic Ejaculations of the
Daily Mind in Transit*

STEVE ABEE

PHONY LID BOOKS
los angeles, california • 2001

THE BUS
Cosmic Ejaculations of the Daily Mind in Transit

Cover photography by Jesse Hopkins

PHONY LID BOOKS
PoBox 29066
Los Angeles, Ca 90029

www.phonylid.com

ISBN: 1-930935-19-6

Library of Congress Control Number: 2001091683

Portions of **THE BUS** have previously appeared in *SIC (VICE & VERSE)* and *PIRATE ENCLAVE*.

PHONY LID BOOKS are edited and designed by Kelly Dessaint and Jesse Hopkins.

First Edition

DISCLAIMER: While this is not a work of fiction, the ideas and suggestions described herein are not to be taken literally, but as one man's speculation on the universe.

for everybody, especially Cat

ECHO PARK AVENUE

I AM WALKING RIGHT NOW, walking down Echo Park Avenue, in Los Angeles, California. Walking, making my way by foot, seeing like I haven't seen before. I am walking and looking and I am listening to my feet bounce off the head of the universal day dreamer, lolly pop wagger and eternity ragger, the big bagger of loose changes, making my way down to Sunset Boulevard, a cross-town bus to catch. Man, it's sweet. It's hot. It's gooey. My neighbor Larry has his binoculars out and is looking into hopefully undressed rooms. There is the Magic Gas Station and the house where the pain in the ass kids live and play and piss you off just to walk by. But, whatever, they are cool.

I am walking, right now, walking in Los Angeles. I have a cross-town bus to catch at Sunset Boulevard. Sweet. Hot. Gooey. Where's the cheese? Trash on the sidewalk, a couch on the curb, stove in the grass, bike frame by the telephone pole, still life. I pass the ranch where they house many roosters, rabbits and sometimes goats, and this amazes me. In the middle of the city, the police academy around the corner, Dodger Stadium next door, freeways on all sides of us, and this ranch... sometimes they even have a horse.

Church across the street, white clapboard, country style, has services at night, and you can hear them singing, mournful, horrible, chanting Jesus-love songs, screaming in Evangelical Spanish, broken English, the unmistakable

7

rhythm and drive of the saved, the convicted, convicted to the bloody flaming lips of Jesus, The Christ, The Savior, The Prince of Heaven, the kind lunatic of fire and peace. The chant is unmistakable, yet understood only by the faithful, and I, walking in the shadow of bamboo and rooster huts, have that faith, know what they are healing, what wound they are sinking into. I know. I try to remember something, but I don't know what it is. I check my pocket, bus cash and keys.

Batey Market at the bottom of the Del Mor apartments. The Batey Market, little market, glass bottles of Coke and Squirt, Hecho en Mexico, childhood, sweet with secrets, sad and delicate secrets, a mystery gas seeps out the door and around the gum stains and the woman on the pay phone, it humps her leg, it climbs the brick wall, it opens the window to the rest of the world, the rest of the world yawns and turns the page, changes the channel, opens a door somewhere, anywhere, all at once. Mystery shapes meaning. There have to be places you see but don't know, that you are in but never own. The woman at the Batey waves.

Scraped faced drunk man, face looking like a flat tire, Asian man reading a ticket the cops just gave him, paint peeling stucco house, windows of wood cracking and grass growing crabby weeds between the cracks of the cement and a sidewalk bent up, broken with roots and a shopping cart in the street. What about gun fire? What about the severe and the bent? Just a shopping cart in the street, kids running around playing tag between the cars, junkies do the hand-off, very serious. But the people at the bus stop don't care. There's a yard full of orange nasturtiums, stray dogs looking for a drink. The streets belong to Mexico, Los Angeles. The hills surround the street, green in the rain, bulging with weed secret lots and groves of mixed trees: Eucalyptus, Pine, Cypress, Pepper and Palm, these hills, bending and burying people in their own backyards, are old. These hills house the freak dreamers. You can feel it. It's hippie like that around here, people making something, a pot of beans, a bucket of chicken, painting faces on the ceiling. It's so pretty with its big dogs and little dogs and little girls in pink mud spot dresses, and good looking girls with fat old men and cowboys staring at them. And I can't help but feel that these hills were something important to the first peoples that lived here, too. You can feel it. You can feel the hills stand up, bend around each other like walruses or sea lions, looking at the sea, watching the city spread out over the plain, cursing the men, blessing the children.

I'm not even thinking. I'm doing something else. I'm swimming. Yeah, that's it, swimming in the brain waves of sparrows and the little super sexo magazine rack across the street, looking for keyholes in the sidewalk, smelling the aromatic curves of the Pioneer Chicken and the Phoenix Express Chinese fast food. House of Spirits, behold that sign of neon, blip-blip clouds of smoke from the house's chimney. It is that time of rush hour day. It is full, full tilt, a whirl spinning in the hands and eyes of the people in the crosswalk: wino, mother, Pep Boys, Homeboy, fine art maker, downtown politico, Raza lover, families piled on top of shopping carts, going to the laundry, people getting tamales at Celaya or fish plates at Pescado Mojado, and some hot looking girl in a mini skirt and a gangster boyfriend, moving like a radio's in her head. And please note that lonesome heavy metal brother, just walking down the street, eloquent destruction in his mind and nothing in his pockets, nothing at all. Buddhist monks in saffron robes waiting for the bus. An old lady walks her granddaughter to the 99 cent store, the little one's mother is in night school, learning English. The bus empties, the neighborhood kid who made it to UCLA gets off the #2, crossed more worlds in that hour and fifteen minute ride than Shakespeare dotted i's, alright. Jeffrey Cruz pop locks in the floodlight spotlight sidewalk grandstand. He goofs, bites it. Cynthia laughs at him, "Haha, you suck." She's his sister. Echo Park, lovely and mean as hell.

The House of Spirits, Pioneer Chicken, Pioneer Market, Pioneer Liquor. There used to be liquor store sidewalks crowded with gunned down ghosts. Kids everywhere, yelling "Fuck you," "Where you going?" from beat up stairways, across the street. Drunks up against the wall, any wall, every wall, drinking, drinking, drinking. Banda falls from a window, somewhere up the stairs, Hip-Hop Seville, one-third paid, booming loud, "69 69... pussy for me and pussy for you," Echo Park behind the wheel.

Blue lights, red lights, yellow lights, just coming on in a full glow sunsetting sky, a drunk eye at the corner, gotta be after five, ECHO PARK AND SUNSET in full tilt bloom, full human dew drips, elote corners, mango sugar sticks, Indian dreams of naked sunlight, Pachuco visions of holocausts, tender youngness in a halter top crossing the crosswalk for days, the tender eyes of love, homework forgotten, popsicles for sucking, while watching the world become the world. Everyone watches. Then they cross and car after car after car goes by.

Karina waves to me, "Mr. Abee…" She took my English class two years ago. She did nothing. It was cool. I wave to Karina and her friend, the sister of all the cholo brothers, who hang out in front of their apartment and stare into every car that passes by, protecting the neighborhood, but the neighborhood still hurts. I have seen young women walk the hot and cruel bright afternoon streets with child, babe in arms and one by a string (some drag them like trophies, others like some heavy things), lonely walking in chanclas, lonely in blue shorts with the sun beating down on them, beating relentless, calm, reminding bright, all the things that are not there. And the billboard cowboy girl laughs because she is safe and can laugh being a billboard, but the face of the mother woman walking alone in her centuries, laughter hurts too far into her belly. She does not do it.

I ask Karina if her brother will draw me something, a tag of my book's name, I want to make a sticker. She says she'll ask. That's good, I say. Her brother is part of a tag banging crew, or at least was. He's good in the heart but rough on the street, like the streets themselves, like the bricks of the walls, the way it is, like the way it is, like the way things can be ugly and just there and you think, or no, you don't think, you just feel, feel that is the way it is and that is it. Like watching fucked-up junkie whore cholas making phone calls outside the New Hollyway bar, drug eyed make up, leering lip stick faces. Somehow it is attractive, their pure brokenness, a siren call. They do their thing on the street, yelling to older gangsters with years of prison ink on their bodies, walking buff guy yelling Rocky Balboa but Echo Park style: "10 Minutes, I'll be 10 minutes." "You better not be fucking around, alright." "You heard what I said." She nods. He drives away gypsy cab and right there on the same sidewalk, sitting next to the doorway to the apartments over the bar are two sweatpants wearing mothers, sitting cross legged and concerned about their children, talking politely about what ever they are talking about and they all occupy the same concrete, see each other and don't care, both doing their destiny, and you ask why should those ladies, just trying to live a good life, have to be on the same street as winos. And you ask why don't the good ladies leave the street and let the winos do their thing? This is Sunset Blvd. Here you don't ask because there is no one to talk to you, no one with answers. It's too late, you shouldn't be out, there is nothing to ask. Shut up. It is the street and all therein, and the bus is coming. Number 4, all the way out to Santa Monica, which is where I need to go. My car is out there, waiting for me.

Three people. Cambodian? Dark Asian? The Philippines? A woman, carrying a plastic bag of stuff, a kid walking ahead of her, a big man, blind, his hand holding onto her, at the shoulder, following behind. She walks cool, no problem, leading the big man across the street, every day.

My car, what about my car? Iron hunk of trouble, the vehicle that moves me personal ways, that I need to get back across town, and then go to work, get groceries in the night, go to the in-laws house for teriyaki chicken and beans, to just pack up the family and cruise somewhere, anywhere, just to get out of the house.

So where is my wife now? My love, my life, my reason, my breath, my oh my, she's staying home with our daughters because like birth and death and masturbation, well, not masturbation, taking the bus across town 15 miles, an hour and a half in street traffic, to pick up your car, must be done alone, 'cause who would want to go with you?

Some people at the bus stop, a Mexican lady and a man in a baseball jacket, check me out, like, "Who goes there?" Or, I think they do, because in the Echo you check to see who is walking down the street. But I think they think, white guy walking on the avenue. I talk paranoid in my head, fight them. "This is where I live. I love these roosters. I celebrate this asphalt and gas station land in lyrical ballad. This ain't no foreign country, this is the goddamn United States of America, and I am the great white citizen of the world."

I damn them, malign their heritage, all to steel myself against their taunts of "Whitey" and "What you doing here?" Which no one says, but it's the kind of shit that I have gotten before, some place, though I am not really sure where. But I know it is in the air, everywhere: you stay in your neighborhood, I stay in mine. Don't cross the line. Everyone is into it. Keep it all separate. Keep the money between all the people. But well, I been crossing the lines all my life. Don't they know? Can't they see? My heart is all about the heart, the heart that beats with you beats with me, and every granule of genetic shadow that haunts you, haunts me, as well.

God Bless you people on the street corner looking at me funny. God Bless you and wherever you are from.

Crazy getting mad at people that I don't even know, but that is the city, that's what you do, trip and smell the stink, crow with the roosters... Okay, those people probably were talking shit. It is the only way to survive with your own mind. You must do it, get into it, explode with rage, suck the addiction down, get into vomit, big bug spray, gutter dust, maggot trash on the corner, let it into your mind, no one is cleaning anything up, so right on, keep walking. Really, I'm just bugged because I have to go across town to get my car. Really, I just had an argument with my wife. The kid started yelling at me too. It's love stuff, and really, this is what the city is filled with. Really, everyone is out here suffering something of the kitchen and bedroom sort, then bringing it on the street, which doesn't care at all. Really, this is the city and all you want you can't have.

We are all citizens of the planet and America is nothing, doesn't exist, without everyone here being illegal. Columbus was a With Out Papers. The very European that brought my family line to this continent, many years ago, stowed away in a barrel to escape some war in Germany. African slaves were stolen and brought here. It's all illegal. Injuns got their land robbed. Illegal. ALL THAT IS COOL ABOUT AMERICA IS ILLEGAL. And of course this is Mexico, everyone here is Mexican. If you live here long enough you become Mexican too, even if you are Chinese.

What about me? What's my problem? I don't have a problem.

The Spirit of America.

A bus comes, but it's not mine.

I am my own nation, my own ruler, my own working class. I got starving masses rioting in my head and they are gonna vomit fire death on you, you, you sonofabitch. Don't come near me with your alternative guitar chords, your glossy dereliction, your knowing smirk...

I don't know, man, my car better be fixed properly. It better work the way it does in my dreams. I take it out to Santa Monica 'cause that's where I bought it, from Hari Pal, the Sri Lankan Hindu Volvo mechanic on Southside Santa Monica, a mechanic that I've known forever. He cuts me good deals on major problems, like this one, a broken head, cracked, 700 dollars from a regular guy, but Hari put it together for 400. So I take the bus for the discount and truth be told, I like going all the way across town on the bus, getting with the stinky and seeing where the head of time is at and maybe I'll see the lovely man Eric Brown.

I don't like cars. I don't like the vehicular reality, the system of car, thus road, thus we all must drive, the fascism of invention. Some genius invents something somewhere so now I have to work my ass off to make sure I can use it. It's not good enough to just be, you got to have invention, you just do. God doesn't care but Exxon do. You can't be part of the world you live in if you don't have a car.

Being stuck in traffic makes your mind ache, cars all over the sky, taillights and exhaust the only thing you can see, walled in, and you don't look at anyone else in their car. No, it's like staring into someone's bedroom window. All these mobile private units, sharing the roadway together, you don't want to look at the person next to you, in

that car, you see too much of them, more than you bar-
gained for, that much is true. And what if they are crazy,
and you flick their switch, and they follow you, want you,
need you, and you have to take radical action? Ah, just
don't look at that next car. But you see I can't help look at
the next car, no one can. Everyone wants to know who is
driving that funky car? Who is going so slow? Oh, hey,
they look good. Maybe that's the one. Oh, I wonder where
they are from? That's a nice car. Look at the old people.
They are so sacred and together in their vehicle that is not
just a car but a carriage of years and commitment. You
can feel their life together, the power of simply sitting
down and watching television with each other, the power
of the very simple things that people do with each other,
the groceries in the back seat of a car, with kids... It is an
awesome sight.

I need my wheels to be somebody, to lift my self out of
the masses, to become one of the chosen, one of the indi-
viduals who choose their own path, brake when they want
to, stop at the K-Mart when they want, go to the post
office then head home. But wait, I forgot to get some
eggs, some film, a tool set, ice. Got to turn around and go
back. And what a good thing to be able to participate at
the In and Out Burger. Yes, this is what it means to drive,
and this is what I need to be, to be a driver, to relax and
drive, to go on through the boulevards of the moon, ask
the wife, "Where do you want to eat tonight? Where do
you want to go tonight? Let's drive down Hollywood Blvd.
Let's see what the lights have to say. Let's see who's walking across the street, getting checks cashed, buying magazines. Who is out there? Who is talking on the pay phone

or to a reflection in the glass window?" And she says, "Okay, get the car seat, get the diapers, get the kids. Let's roll, baby. Let's go drive to the airport and watch the planes take off and make out beneath the airplane exhaust, while the babies sleep in the backseat."

My bus comes. I get on. Squeeze through the crowd, saying, "Excuse me, excuse me," moving to the back, past all the people who don't want to sit in the back because the seats are sideways and you have to stare at other people, and there are crazy people in the back, if not now, then later. Whacked out jailbirds talking to the girls they have tattooed on their arms, "Baby, I wanna lick you, baby, I am gonna lick you." And then zzzzzz, zonked out, head on the seat. I find myself a seat right by the back door. I check to see if the seat is wet. You never know, a wino could have wet his pants downtown, got up, dreaming drunk about something but forgot, felt his piss wet ass, got sad, real sad. "Fuck, how come I did that? Now I'm all wet." But so drunk the feeling never makes it out of his eyes, he stumbles off the bus, onto Broadway, down to an alley, and pukes in a box, and thinks about when he used to play baseball in high school. "I was good looking." The seat's not wet though.

I look around: people. Yes, people, sunlight through the window, yes sunlight, sunlight on the people. Yes, how nice, how sun shiny. The sun is kind, the sun is truly kind, and the sun is brutal, and the sun is sad. The sun is the tooth, the bone, the pig's nose, the poison blow, the venturer of naked storms that blow across the mind of mind in gutter secret caves of liquor store prophets. Those who you see only once, crying to themselves beneath the big sign in the parking lot, "Love, Love is the truth, that's all there is." Crying to someone, but no one is around. They smell bad. You turn away and then look back and they are gone. And the sun nods, like it does now. The sun says nothing, just falls down on these heads, nodding. The sun, just people in the sun, the cloth of flesh, the brow of rivers, just people, nothing, just everybody and their universes humming with the jet streams that hold us here between too far and too close to the sun. Nothing, just people exploding silent volcanic bus ridden galactic. The hands of stars, the arms of deserts, the body of engines, bellies of fruit, the navels of spines, the lips of long skies, dark skies.

Oh, the eyes of eyes. Eyes carrying rivers of eyes, eyes that have seen the world around three thousand times, eyes that look on tomorrow as the day they are going to die, eyes that wish to kill something, someone, but never will, eyes that cheat and eyes that wish they loved someone well enough that they would not have to lie, eyes afraid of being anything, so they stare into the cinder blocked wall of nothing and that is what they become, eyes of those who have laid awake all night for no reason besides the sound of the ocean coming through their walls. The eyes that have stared down on the face of love, leaving in the morning, off to work, now been gone the whole day, and now they are coming back. Those eyes of love, eyes that saw the baby's heart beat, eyes that put the child to sleep. The eyes that met the eyes of the web builder as it built the body that was the body that came into his eye.

I look out the window, turn from imagining what everyone is thinking, thinking, man, that's just what you are thinking. And I think that is true, too. I see a sign for mayor and think about politics. Politics does not ride this bus. There is no government that governs this ride. This ride, like this city, is on another planet. Forgotten, not heard, only felt when burning. Everyone knows that we are in the middle of the biggest camera eye on the globe, but no one is looking at this ride, not here... there is no President of the United States, of Mexico, Philippines, CIA dictator of Cambodia, subsidized banana lords.

This city is underground, it is the ground, the street in my head. It is in the backyard beneath the junked car, beneath the pile of laurel leaves, or eucalyptus, or any other tree that came here, that was here, that flourishes, that makes smog. It is some kind of human thing, purely human, human without body, human soul. It is silent, a bubble of breath waiting to explode, the spiky head of dandelion seeds waiting to blow off into a parking lot. This city of Angels, under god, under-fed, under the eyes of Guadalupe, under the hands of the Santerea Saints, where everyone prays and everyone knows that Mother Teresa is in heaven, a Saint, that saints are real, more real than presidents... but even they do not change the course of this world.

But do they not make the world turn a different direction? The sun a different shade? Windows into the other side? Geysers of the dream beneath the wheels of sun and moon and stars and rings of Saturn? Jesus sang on the cross, right before his lungs collapsed and his ribs broke trying to breathe and the wound in his side, dripping water, turned into a home for flies and their eggs. Yes, he sang that song, and the sun cried from the holy side crumbling beneath the weight of this world's sorrow, lonely, not heard—Buddha vomited under the Bo berry tree.

There are no politics on this bus, just the world, no elections, only time infected with breath, with blood, meaning this: everything is necessary. All the fingers on my hand, all the streets and words we pass through. The tired lined face of the mestizo man, looking at his necessary hand, holding a baseball cap, stained from stained hands, could be anything grease, is anything grease, engine grease, cooking grease, society grease, street grease, 99 Cent grease, time grease, grease from the springs running the clocks, the grease of dollars, the grease of value itself, this man's hands are covered with the grease of pure economy: work for your right to breathe, pure cause, the effect is this life, these walls, this bus, that light, the faces, the faces and hands, the president, the saints, and these words, effluvia, what do they mean? It sounds like words flying out the window, lost change landing heads up, vapor rinds of an earthly fruit.

These words stuck to my shoes, rolling around the bus floor like empty cans, rattling planetary vocabularies, language is the garbage talking, the pools of sweat, the streams of blood that have attached themselves to my own veins, infections of grease and need, the grease of the world is need. And the man in front of me, staring out the window, seeing everything, seeing nothing, seeing that he is going home, yes, that he is alive and alive means work. Work keeps the world going, keeps the Angel with wings, keeps the dollar on its horse, the horse on the streets, the streets in his hand, and his hands dirty, the engine must keep running, love and hate, simple, old, true. The cylinder exploding with sparking octane, kicking the horse over and over again, and this man, standing next to me, staring out the window, with thousands of years in his eyes, he holds that horse and all this shit in his hand. It's just there, he isn't even grabbing. We all do when we bleed, everyone on this bus. This is a big bus, and this bus is full with waiting minds inside of the mind of one eye that never closes as long as we do not close, because that is our own eye, the flower of our need, held in our own hand, the grease of our blood. And here blooms the flower, here bloom the ashes, here bloom the echoes of shadows, the ringing of streets from subterranean consciousness, places no eye has seen, because we can never see where we were born.

ALVARADO STREET

THE BUS STOPS AT ALVARADO and the bus driver watches the people get on. The bus driver, she is kind like the sun, taking us through the world. It is 5:30pm on October the 2nd. Rosh Hashanah starts now, and I want everyone to know. Alvarado bus stop scene: gold tooth white lady, dressed in black, carrying a child sized black ventriloquist dummy, talking to a floppy converse wearing, grease monkey jump suit Mexican guy, her husband, man, companion, whoever, is standing smiling approvingly at whatever she is saying. What is she saying? The husband is a kimono wearing gray haired guru, pony tail man, Evangelical Millennial Hippies freaked on a Santerea Alvarado I Ching, throwing bones in the aisle: face tired, hard, crazy looking on the zoom in. Are they prophets? Do they have a following? Does the dummy doll speak the illumined verse, administer all cures? I put my money on that one. Alvarado is that kind of street. The bus takes off.

There is a billboard for a new Ranchero Radio station. Luscious Mexican city/country style girlie, laughing, "Come and dig me." The background a yellow as bright as lust upon the haze, making hated love to the overcast light dripping orange smog. It is too much. Her tits are full and out, not porno popping but cowgirl style. She's got a laughing face, laughing 'cause she knows she is safe. Like I said before, this sign is immoral. It will make my wife jealous, will make me feel bad, will be funny. It is funny, her sexy goofy leering lipstick marked mouth, her country smile fills the sky and the bus. Who is she? She's got meat. This is wonderful. She is all over the city. Wherever a Mexican cowboy might be. I am a Mexican cowboy. I am lonely for my land and my horse, my love and my domain, and she promises me a happy dance. There is rebellion in her lips, mouth wide, the rebellion of good times in a crooked world. Mexican honky tonk revolution on the first world radio, quebradita break down and love me on the hay. Ahh hell, it's just a billboard and I feel insane and wonderful because it's turning me on so much, taking me out of my mind so much. I am so full of sex that I can't even stand myself. I am hard to love, but I love fully. I love the girl on the billboard.

The billboard good time gal stays behind, waiting to seduce someone her size, and I am sitting quiet with my mind going through my hands, out the window, down the stairs, around the world and the sun, getting burned by the lustful tongue of the day, the fat worm of being, the big plum of mamma sky. My hands are in some tomb of wealth and stature, in a marriage that will end in disaster, in a hand that will never leave me, making love and love to please me. My hand is burning in the persecutor's fire. My hand is the hand of a liar. My hand is fixing a pipe that the city didn't know it had.

Foster's Freeze and the street my wife grew up on. Oh, lovely Cathy, how I love to ride with thoughts of you stuck to the window of my bus. How I love to see the Frisbees of your dreams and stories circling each other in the sky, how I love to love you, baby, how I love to hold you, and make my life and children with you, how I love the things you are, the streets you have loved and the places you have been, right here, how I love the way the street you grew up on goes up the little hill, Waterloo, you are my Waterloo, there your mother and you and sisters lived. You, sleeping in the living room with your mom, while your sisters got the bedroom, you, good girl in Catholic school, doing your homework between day dreams of cloud berry vacations that lasted so long you never got older, and you walking on your knees up the hill, forced by the bully who later got brain damage, karmic retribution for fucking with an angel, he messed with you and the spirits did the job. How I love your stories of Catholic school, the hippie nun who made you all learn John Denver songs and the story where you and your cousins were singing like you were in the Wizard of Oz going down to Alvarado to buy candy from Kings Liquor. Years later we go in there and the guy still wants to sell you candy, but we buy booze instead. Oh, I wish I was a fly on the hand that helped you tie your shoe. Shoo fly. You'd say, "Hey this damn fly won't leave me alone." You'd say, "This fly is slobbering all over me." You'd say, "Hey this fly is kinda cute." Or maybe I'd be a bird, or a dog, or just be thinking about you on the bus. Oh, I love you woman who was the girl who got in trouble at Catholic school for bringing Vanity to record share day and still is… you are the genius of all.

We are insane, my love, we did insanity to each other, we just jumped into each other, unzipped and said here: take my ravines, my queen, be my Gasoline, burn my city with me and let's get the river around us and swim full of

nights and eyes into the tantrum of our tears, let's be pup-
pets to our strings, let's be walls to our music, let's not
make no sense and do what the knife says, cut it down,
become none and then another and make humans and
build a road with our lives out into the never ever sea and
there I will see you and you will see me. What have we
done? What are we doing? Where are we going? Husband
and wife, married, with a kid, two kids, "Don't worry, I got
a plan, we will have stuff, Publisher's Clearing House will
find us."

Wow, we destroyed each other, we came into each
other's lives like competing storms, annihilated our beings
for the other, endured the other's rages for our love,
endured the most frightening belly of soul opening love.
We annihilated our beings with each other, never has there
been a love so fascist, so pure, so demanding, so necessary, so not in my life, not in yours, not in the man buried
in the desert sand. We are insane, deeply corny and holy,
mad at nothing and in love on the sub atomic particle
exploding in the stellar iris of a honey bee, we have given
each other a cancer, a death wish, an until death wish,
something gone beyond mind, voices, lives talking in our
sleep, you know what I am talking about: When we first
started sleeping together, we would be falling asleep after
making love and talking to each other, not our voices, but
something else, some kind of voice inside, not talking
with words but with waves, waves that were talk, like
winds blowing light into and through each other, 'cause
when we would wake we would snap out of the voices,
and not hearing them, realize, and say, "Hey, were we just
talking to each other?"

So then you left for Mexico and we drank all the night before, got underwear drunk, you mixing some good whiskey cocktails, the next day my head was a bad thing, bad, alcohol limping love brain, a delicate thing, full of a curing love, a curing love... My friends, she left on an afternoon airplane, it was a nice might rain day, and I watched from the street on the hill next to the beach, overlooking the runways, the Pacific Ocean all over the sky, hangover had subsided into that euphoric state where you are floating, light and redeemed, slightly fucked up even. I watched her plane take off, out and over the sea, rising high and turning left, dune weeds blowing, and the seashore down below. I felt alive for the first time, felt gods smiling, felt Angels, felt the dogs of hell baying at my good eye, felt the sun come out from behind a cloud where it had been hidden all day long, it came out and it shined, shined like sun shines when it is telling you something, simply saying yes and yes it was, and yes it is, and I went home with yes all over my body and falling out of my hair and as I burnt my steak on my little stove in my little apartment, a morning dove lit down in the window. Too much. What is going on? I wondered. A dove at night? The dove of love, a love-sent dove, landing in my window? "Would you like something to eat?" I asked. Startled, it flew away.

I love you, woman, eyes with life all around you, it was sadness brought us together, it was sadness made us understand the voices in our sleep. The sweet flower of sadness unwrapping us in the wine bottle dark, sweet, sweet sadness. Weep in the arms of the forever ocean. The life we have is the work of the feathers, of the sword. It is not simple or easy or even kind, but it is simple, it is easy. It is tantrum, it is love, it is sorrow, it is everything that has made us and everything we will make. I'm so goddamn heavy with it. The fact is I recognized your smell from another life. I perceived destiny when I held you. It was deep as the river of blood that we all pretend isn't there everyday beneath our feet.

The streets hold the directions of the four Zoas, William Blake is the crossing guard, the blood of Abel calling in the crosswalks, we weep for our sins of original murder, killing our own face, the faces of our young, the street is a bed of nails and tears, on which you cannot rest, the curbs are harbors for garbage and ghosts, the faces of the wasted lives, the never lived, and the very nearness of all their voices, all their blood, the sky hears it, the birds hear it, the Lotus knows it, Gabriel blows his horn that we must atone, begin again, listen to the voice of blood talking on telephone lines across time, this, the storm drain of Eden, running back into the dark firmament, but we all will get off long before that. This is the exhaust vision of John Divine, John Future, this is the mangled hallucination of a paper bag bottle of exhaustion, graffiti smiles, TRUSTY MINOR CHILD, ALSO, BEGONE. Delilah X rants in her sidewalk tombstones looking for clues.

I watch the stores go by and I think about the things that are inside: dog food, soap, cigarettes and aspirin, drink and grog. I look at the storm drains and I think of the Los Angeles River, when I was taking the train, the Amtrak to San Diego to look at the book that was being made of my words, passing into East Los Angeles and I saw the homeless houses inside the defunct cat face storm drains, a ramshackle fence of boxes crowned with green bottles shining in the sun setting winking eyes of glass lizards, a man, sitting in a chair reading and talking to a woman getting up and walking into the interior of their home, the tall mouth of the drain and above them flew an American flag, America, by the river bum bottles of dry drains, rippling in the wind, flowing, very much like a picture, so real that I saw it a million times before, and it flew over these lives, across the sleeping heads of us on the train. The day was like it is today, almost over, and the lives of these people, a couple, and they were sitting in the mouth of a storm drain, with a life clearly laid out.

The place was their own, the flag flew a funny faced thing, the joke of America, the failure of America, and somehow I felt something else too, not horror, but happiness, this was the success of America, I was happy, people had fashioned a life outside of telephone lines, even if they didn't want their destitution. I was happy that they were courageous enough to live, even if they were not living, they were there and I saw them, outside of society, in this world of complete catalogues, where secrets die the minute they are breathed between the glasses and the sheets of love, where everything has a champion and everyone knows everything, where nothing is true, real, possible. I marveled, I envisioned, I left the moon, to see people living so impossibly with a big American flag flying, I felt somehow they were doing it for all of us, they were living their destitute life, victims, perpetrators, drunks, sharp minded, college educated, drop outs, wife beater, AIDS victim, abuser, addict, killer, dead. It did not matter what they were or did, they were all these things and they were living on the side of the river because in

this cosmic mind that we create daily and that creates us
nightly, someone must exist beyond the tentacles of reason as it is mandated by the freeway to shopping mall to
prefabricated home to work and back again model of
modular existence.

No, go then, yes then, someone is beneath it all and the
sun, and for that I salute them, no address, no known
place of existence, next to the thin trickles of concrete
river, in the belly of Los Angeles, where the sun is dust,
draped desire hands, floating in serene horror down onto
the weeded train tracks, and I must explode because my
soul is big here, too big here for my breath, my lungs, my
skin, my veins, I must explode a million diamond eyed
tears across all the heads of hair and the pomegranates of
love, the fruits of abuse, the tender eyes of want, the fluid
of this sphere's sunflower destiny.

Sunset Blvd., in the electric underwater sunlight at the
beginning of fall, the Hebrew New Year, because they are
a planting people, the fall of the year, the fall of time, the
fall of something I thought I was. Really, who am I now?
Where am I going now? I didn't die at 27. I am falling, I
am the fall of falling, my life is ending on this bus and I
am a family man and I am a city man, and I am a cosmos
man and I am a lonely man, full of people getting off
work and unfit to work anywhere, ever… the lady who got
on the bus with me back at Echo Park and Sunset, skinny
and mean, face tired of being part of her body, clothes
tired of hanging from her bones, sunglasses tired of being
so dark, she sits behind mirrorshades not smiling, not seeing, programmed by her need to follow the street to
Silverlake and get off and walk into Thomas Burger

Number One and make a phone call and wait. Her hands hold gnarled air, cramped with waiting, she drips something you don't want to look at onto the floor. Is it blood? I wish it were. I wish she was bleeding to death right in front of me. That would be better than having to watch her seeping slowly apart, like everyone doesn't know that she is insane and high and going to get more high.

The blouse she is wearing has a little bow on the collar and long sleeves, the pattern is Holly Hobby checks and her lips are painted a subdued red, her lips are cracked a sour pucker and she is wearing an overcoat, and it is hot, warm, a balmy night, a humid day, the best hours for love, where while you are fucking you sweat but not too much, just enough to be aware of your bare ass and the window that is open and the breeze that is making you cold and your love partner, your love and you become a muscle in the breeze of the afternoon and your sweat, a muscle of being, pumping to sweat out the seed of your soul, her soul, all soul, I hope she is on birth control, or not, 'cause this come is gonna win, yes that kind of sweaty breeze, but not now, now she is cold, because she is dying, her blood is dying in her veins and she has to give it a drop of chemical for it to recall how to live, recall through the miles of poison that she has dropped into herself.

I am sorry for her, I hope she has killed the demon that chased her into this bus, onto this street, made her get off at Silverlake and make the call, and wait, wait for someone slightly less fucked up than her to breathe some life into her limp blood. I hope she killed that demon. But I know she didn't. It's okay, she can't feel it. It's okay. It's cool. I'm happy. Hope you are too.

Don't you want to get stupid like that? Come on. Get therapy, join the program, get wisdom, somehow, but don't you want to get high and be gone from it all and still be alive? I want to get high like that, make the world disappear, make the sky never sunny nor dark, just my enemy, that's all. You know I do. As much as I love my life, my left lung wants to breathe amphetamine wine clouds. Lay out a rail right here and I'll do it, swim to see the land of the lost, let the world consume me, the tide of disease, face like chalk, vitamin pills, become a broken levee, war pig spilling demon seed all night, driving, the roof leaking, the sun chasing me across the sky, a fist full of happiness, get me alright, chattering to the bathroom wallpaper moons, electric messengers in my teeth, bugs in my hair, I want your mad antennae in my eye. You know I'd do the dust. But I won't because I have things to do and I have people to be and I've got lives living all over me and that is why I cannot. Do not freak. I have a car to get.

SILVERLAKE BOULEVARD

THE SKINNY WOMAN, MIRRORSHADES REFLECTING in the bus window, she rings the bell. It is her stop: Sun Lake Drugs, neon lit square letters, The Cafe Tropical, The Silverlake Lounge, Drag Bar, rock and roll lou-ow, Corinas Tacos, sidewalk taco carts, LaunderLand, The COLDEST BEER IN TOWN, Usulutan Pupusas... she walks away, and I salute her, lost, too, outside of the sweeping arc of the klieg lights, and all she ever wanted was to be loved but she is not loved, only lost, and sometimes that is as close as we can get, with or without someone else. She is in my head, now, in my shoes, I say something for her, quietly, a prayer, she doesn't need it or want it, I do it anyway. Good night.

Silverlake Lounge. One night me and the family were driving around and we pulled up in front of the Lounge, the curtain was open and we could see the stage and the singer on that stage, and she saw us and sang to us in our car. She, an old Mexican transvestite, pot belly, love and smoke wrinkled eyes, lipstick all over her face, singing like crying, crying something like years, fierce years, fierce eyes, hand raised in defiance of all that cannot be true but needs to be... singing her varicose heart out, an empty bar, and it was cold. Was it cold? It should have been. Someone with a horn in eternity blew her a note, gave her a brush, let her in, and she pointed, "I see you, I see you."

Oh, sweet soul, tender flesh of eternity that you hold

within the breath of your blood, the very real dog of nowhere that leads through the forests and down to the sea, this dog that is the forest, that is the sea, that is the footsteps in your head, the window sill filling with the junk of meaning's strange menagerie: the pants of being are being unbuttoned by the nighttime, naked ass in the sky, cock in the moon, as the sunset wets the western sky with vagina designs, open your eyes to the eyes of eyes. God has no religion. Love has no scene. Life has no cage.

The bus keeps going. It is full of people. The guy next to me smells. He is drunk, a guy, young, touching a woman's hair like it is a fine lace thing he has never seen before. She moves gently away from him, pretending he isn't there and then he goes away like he isn't there, but he is there, sitting down now by the back door.

Light has a mind of its own, acts different all the time. Perhaps it is that the basin is so wide and long, that you get shelves of clouds and roofs of good sky, streaks of smog, like lines of a potter's wheel, clouds of billowing heaven like in some Michelangelo God painting, pillars of fiery looking smog that only something evil could have made and something evil did make it and I live here any-way, and through this the light moves, the delicate textures of cancerous angelic shades splitting into the prism of a bee's eye as it surrounds your hands, so you can be on the bus, at sunset time, looking at the aisle, the heads of the people bobbing with the sway of the bus and this sight reveals something, something, I don't know what, I don't know the word, it is a bunch of words, many words, words floating through the haze, bursting little fish egg bubbles around our ears, in our hair. It is the way light holds all of us, today, right now, on this bus, holds us like it wants to take us apart, like it wants to tell us something about our blood vessels, like it wants to unstring the neuron cables that surround our bones, that guide our indexes of weather and fear and tie these ropes of electric being together. Today the light is green, with blue shadows…

The dogs bark at the fence of the auto garage that is someone's soul. A bearded wino sings on the cement curb at the Coin-Op Car Wash. He sings therefore there are trees and birds in those trees and sex going on in the rooms of the apartments surrounding the street and a man smoking a cigarette out the window of his room, which is above the Siete Mares seafood restaurant, he is there and because of him an airplane flies by and he thinks about flying, and there are families sitting and eating and I know that it is good, have eaten there many times, kind of want to stop now and eat, it is nice now, the bullets are not flying on the corners where the bullets fly and the spray paint is idle in the hands of the doomed. The bald headed lovers of doom, Aztlan Trece, are not apparent, only their jailed names are written on the forget-me-not-walls and it is all so tragic and dramatic and endless. Fish tacos. Fish tacos. What fish do you catch on Sunset and Vendome? What fish do you catch on this street? Is it a fish at all? What can the living tell you where the panhandlers hang out in the car wash, the one I was talking about, the one where the wino is singing? He is still singing, singing crazy, gravel eyed, bad sound, while some other local flavor type has his pick up truck parked there, stuffed with the insane accumulation of destitution. People who have nothing have so much in their cars. And he sits there, never washing his car, never moving, just walking around, across the street to get a coke, down the street to buy some cigarettes, yelling at people who stare at him, "Hi—What the fuck do you want?" Swear to God.

Yes, Goddamn it, yes, God love it, fish tacos are good at that place. And the families sit, watching the cars go by, wondering about things and talking about other things, wondering about money things and talking about other things, wondering about universe things and then talking about the universe with a french fry in one hand, and then holding hands and the children run out into the street shouting the hosannas of ashes, the psalms of the lion as he opens his jaws to roar the darkness of eternity, yes the children wrap themselves around street lamps and run and jump from apartment buildings, mass hysteria and suicide.

I join them. I take off my clothes and jump around in a good time circle, marking the spot I wish to be abducted from but no one comes and I quit my weird day dream and look back at the bus and know that what I really wish for is to be sitting there eating a fish taco but I am on the bus and the bus is going to the ocean and I must pick up my car so that I will not ride the bus, fish taco, but I continue in the underwater sun of a wine dark sea and relish my life in the bus line of the valley of search and I know that I have been on this bus since before the wheel got hold of the ground, since forever let go of the wheel and time started to drip down from the hole in the middle of my eye. That's what I'm saying, listen up! I saw this bus fill up and I saw it empty. I was here when all our parent's parent's parents first got on, I saw your mother in her window seat looking out at tomorrow land, feeling her belly and wondering how wide the sorrow of suburban skies could be. And I saw your old man with his biblical cane come down like a lot of spiritual concrete into her life, I saw that, I saw them bend each other into hearts and broken megaphones. I saw you get on as a babe, an embryo, an egg that had not been lit by falling desire, and I see myself, yes, in the hands and hair of my parents, dressed hip, dad in a cool suit and tie, mom in a sleeveless dress, it's hip, my parents look great, only they aren't my parents, they are two people at a party in 1965, in the Hollywood Hills, it is a small gathering for Thanksgiving and my dad is saying something funny and tilting his head and smiling a half smile, hiding his crooked teeth and cute as all tomorrow and today, my mother laughs and looks at her drink, thinking of something to say. What can she say? She is in love, she says nothing, she says, "STEVEN CHRISTIAN ABEE IS IN YOUR BALLS. ONLY I KNOW THE SEED. ONLY I GOT THE EGG."

And I see myself get off, old, bones crumbling, frail, longing to be dust with the air, so tired of life and love and death, so ready to go, I see that old man and I want to grab his coat, sit him down, find out what went on, how did his fingers become so worn and lovely like the street on a rainy quiet afternoon where the cracks all fill with water and the miracles play marbles on tombstones in your hair. I grab for him, and his coat turns to dust and he turns to dust and it all just flies away. Haha. The bus stopeth not.

We have been on this bus much longer than we know and this bus has been on this ground much longer too. This city of angels seems a young place. The numbers are small here, but this city is built on old, old ground, old and evil, the tribes knew this, they knew this land would rise to destroy those who dared it to come alive. It is a menacing ground, full of drought, fire, pestilence and sunshine, with open arms, knowing our weaknesses, our need for promises, ground so old it is subterranean, it is an ancient bed of seas that just rose Leviathan-like to the surface to breech and begin its migration again, the migration of the world, the world to this edge of land, it is evil.

What is evil? It allows, it lets us do what we want, even die, and that is evil, that is the devil, never betraying his promise to give, freedom, freedom is evil, knowledge is evil, life is evil, God is evil, the sacred is evil, love is evol spelled backwards. This ground is bad, it causes chaos in the mind, it deserts you at the last minute, always leaves you alone, this ground is alive and in the latest hour, when the dark splinters and shines, the old ground speaks through every brick, glass, girder, stoplight, taco truck, cop car, bumcart, troubled cerebellum beehive… a lament that breathes and breaks the compass of time, time so weak, it cannot count what is being done, it cannot count the signals of the earth, not now or any now, ever. Time is more temporary than its smallest click. The earth here is old and it rolls down the street in rabbit moon winds, rolls down our arms, electric tongues, cactus eyes, wind, the stuff of pressure, hot and cold, the stuff of voices heard and not heard.

The earth here, it will not let go. It menaces the concrete walls, the roof tops, the buildings that have scrawled themselves into the ground. It breaks up around them, cracking the asphalt with weeds, the dry air aging the facades, man is temporary, says the Dandelion Queen. Time is temporary, but desire is forever and I have it all right here, and the sky, the very large sky nods its head, surely, seen it all, seen it coming all along, seen it coming, The Oregon Trail, Mayflower, Middle Passage, Jerusalem Crusade, seen the sane world coming mad, seen the sane world build towers and speedways, cars, but the cars don't work without a road, build a road, road the world, build bombs, but the bombs don't work without a war, build a war, war for the whole world, build hunger, but the hunger won't work if everyone is fed, build famine so the world can hunger—behind the lights of reason insanity lies, deceives, hunts without mercy for companions, bleeds needlessly, follows the fevers of the sorcerers of concrete, but the ground knows who owns what and who owns the clock and who is old and who is who. That's right. The ground knows.

The hills cradle the boulevard and the tangle of trees tangle up the stairs and shade someone's backyard, who knows who, and who cares, this backyard is a heaven place in my head, a place where one sits in a lawn chair with relaxing beverages and watches the world unfold into the sky and the tree and the bush speak calmly to you, at thy feet and in this unfolding comes a clock from somewhere, a different kind of clock, a clock counting in all directions and in all manner of time: static time, fluid time, muscle counted time, psychic time, time marked off in ages of clay bells and wild feathers, time counted in leaves of flame, time as it is scrawled on the bleached bones of the forgotten dead, time webbed into the recesses of mind and belching out almost physical visions, memories of excellence and despondence, and in this sea of time you love yourself, lost body crying over who knows what. "What's wrong?" she asks, and you can't answer her. You just wave your hand and say something about the clouds but it is too horrible, this ocean that ripples around your feet, it is swallowing you, it is loving you, saturating your veins. "It is a nice evening," you say, and she nods, "Yes." She understands, she knows that the sky has come undone, the horizon has split your eye wide open and made you drink. She touches you, you dissolve.

She understands and this is why we are married. This is why we had one child and now have another, this is why you feel like becoming her in the bones while making love, this is why you are happy and being happy in this fucked up world is just not normal, ain't cool, not possible, must be blown up, can't happen to you, so you say, "Go away, don't bug me." And she is sad at this and you are sad at this, and you are reassured by this disappointing sadness, you feel at home, not so naked, nothing is open, the ocean in your mind has closed and all your clothes are on, and the sky of eternal time is just a place for airplanes and smog, now, and you know that you have lost the ticket to the other side again and you know that you have lost the moment of naked sea bones, and you know she knows, and you look at her and you reach out to touch her, apologize, make up a story, an explanation of some sort about something, something that you ate, just the way you are, something that you had to do today that got stuck in your ass, something that someone said, you know the world of a million somethings that you always go to when you don't know the fucking reason for anything, you say something from that world, pull out one of the cards from that file and read, and she knows you are full of shit, but that it is not your fault and she lets your shirt dry her tears and you hold each other, and you laugh because you are fucked up like all the fucked up stuff, you laugh and it is beautiful, laughing, she cries, you cry but somewhere else, back in 3rd grade, back in your third grade dust, you cry and here in this world, this sliver of time, you laugh and it is cool. You pour out the drink, the kid cries, you go to her, you hold her, all three of you in the magic triangle of the primal family, the magic number three and you hum in your bones and you see in the eyes of your love that there is the sea you were seeing, it never left, never went anywhere, never got lost, you are just so deep in the water you think it is air.

So breathe deep, motherfucker, and drown, once and for all, just drown and be alive, drown, drown in the soft sauce of seducing night, and now you really want to fuck, now you really want to let your river flow into the sea, get Edenic fish flowing out of your balls, into the nest, get real again, and you know and I know, she knows, the walls, and the trees, and the dirt lot weeds know that is why you got so much fuck on your mind, she undoes you, she unzipped me, pulled me down into nectar walls unimagined and lit the sky impossible with cherry bombs and rose water and turned me into a starry tree of orgasm leaves, wanting all the woman that the world is because I found my woman, whose hands hold the sea, the earth, the moon, the orbits of deep golden things and we sing and I can't let go. I want the sky, the earth, learning a time that I will never be able to tell, but will always feel, the billboards of lust stand all over the world and they love me, and I love them, because I love her and all of it, and it is love all the time, love all the time, riding on this bus thinking about the dreaming and the fucking and the humming of the engine making my blood run round my bonedaddy-day and I am riding on the bus of fuck, the bus a phallic vehicle piercing the city and we are all splitting seeds and spilling with cum, sticky on our shoes—that is why no one is talking to each other, that is why we are all quiet. We are high in the bus of angel muscled engines. I look around, think about yelling something, but don't.

SANBORN AVENUE

CRUISING THROUGH THE COLORFUL STOREFRONTS of Silverlake, past the groovies and gone freaks of Circus of Books, past the most beautiful street. I look down the street, the lights spread out, McDonald's on the Horizon, donuts in the night, yogurt in neon, Detour man love bar, Jiffy Lube next door. Funny, I think, laugh and look a little nuts, I am sure, because I am laughing, but that's good.

I see a young kid, raggedy walking down Sunset, crossing the Myra Street bridge. There's a nice view of the city right there. Not the whole city, but you can see a horizon stretch of rooftops and how the mountains curve around. The sunsets are nice to watch from that spot. If there are clouds it is a nice spot because you can see enough sky to watch them wrap around in the sky, but really it is a nasty bridge with freaky monster people living on the side in the vacant lot tall trees, and when you stand there someone is bound to stop and hit on you for sex, and people walking by look at you funny because they think you are out there waiting to get picked up. But sometimes I stand there anyway and I think of Mateo.

Mateo was a fucked up delinquent with his brain on sideways. I first met him at the Onyx cafe where I was hanging out at the time. His mom was one of the locals. She was a crazy communist fanatic who became a radical psychic and then discovered that she was Native American. When I say discovered, I mean she ate some mushrooms in the desert and had a vision in which an Indian came to her and told her where she was from.

I met Mateo when he was coming out of juvenile detention. He was whack and talking shit and writing poetry. I told him I liked the poetry and so I was his friend. But the thing was he was too much, you know, "bitch" and "fuck" and "ho" and kickin' ass and all that, and lonely as fuck. You could see his eyes wobble in the hollow. So then, whatever, I don't see him for a while, I go through my own problems, a relationship I am in is ending, I am getting heavy into speed again, and I am in school, my last two quarters at UCLA. So what? I don't know, I don't know, I am on this bus, talking to myself and I don't know... background, I guess.

So I am down at the Oki Cafe, on Hollywood Blvd., eating an Oki Burger and farting. Those things fucked up my bowels, but I loved them. He's walking around selling some books he stole from his mom's house. He hates his mom. Why not? She goes from the Spartacus League Commies to some Dark Minded New Age Psychic. Anyway, I see Matt and I don't have any drugs. I want some drugs. I have some schoolwork to do, which I have put off, or do I? I can't recall. Maybe I just wanted to get high... anyway, I say, "Hey, man, do you know where I can get some zip, or something?" I was always trying to come up with clever names for it. He called it tweak, and said down on the Blvd., where all the runaways hang, he knew where to hook up. So I went with him. I drove him down there and we drove by a bunch of places. He asked some English girl standing on the corner if she knew where to get some tweak and she was all not now but in a couple days, and she was into him, and I saw right there that the whole world was on drugs. Then we parked and went looking for some street kids that he knew from working down on the Blvd. A whole crew hanging, talking to some social worker, all kind of kids, black, white, punk rock, hip hop, girl, boy… The leader was this good looking, smart as hell, black kid. And there was this little white girl with a big backpack and really bad cough, and this other black guy, dressed nice, but so high, he didn't know where the sidewalk started but he followed everyone alright anyway, twisting and spider crawling on stairs that weren't there.

We just went walking and knocking on a whole bunch of doors. I didn't even think, "What am I doing here?" I wanted drugs and I didn't care. I was letting my own thing go. Let me just say this, not to say I was all fucked up and that, but I was all fucked up. After about an hour of walking around Yucca apartments we ended up at Wilcox and Yucca. This kid, the leader guy, he knew this frazzled 40 year old white lady who was sitting on a car talking with someone. I waited across the street with Matt. The guy went over, came back, explained the situation, I gave some money, like ten dollars, got a bag, it tasted right, cut, but still drugs.

So me and Matt went back to my house, did some drugs and he was talking all crazy, "I know I am the deliverer," or something like that. "I am with this girl, I put my fingers in her pussy and made her eyes roll back, made her come. Now if I can do that, I can do anything." "Yeah, yeah you can," I said, thinking about another line and this crazy person in my apartment. "The universe, there is a fight between the great black father and the bitch, the white bitch, inside of the wheel in the center of sky, you see that is where he lives, and he must silence her with his dick. He has the magic in his dick, but she is powerful, she can change into things, she can become things that she wasn't."

I was high, and he was freaking. I didn't want to be around him anymore, he was tripping too hard. I didn't want to be around anyone. I had work to do. I had a paper to write for Shakespeare Class, on *The Merchant of Venice*. I started seeing little cubicles of thought that Shylock was living in, some kind of mental social bondage that he made for himself because of the role society demanded from him. And Matt was sitting there, talking and talking his mad cosmology.

I took him home. I didn't care what he was gonna do. His eyes were shaky, like they were falling away from his bones, from his face. Too much, the kid was too much. I dropped him off and went back to my work, where I tweaked out, dripping pages of mayhemic interpretation. I got an A in the class. I saw Matt about a week later at a party, and he was flipped. He thought he was Jesus. No, he KNEW he was Jesus.

"Wouldn't you rather know Jesus than Matt?" "No." He picked up a book I had called *Jesus Through the Centuries* and took it saying, "I got to find out about myself." He was too sad and lost. It was over. The next time I saw him he had shaved his head and he started hanging out in front of the Onyx Cafe pouring dish soap and sand and tap water and any other crap he could find into a container and methodically lighting a candle over it and dripping the wax into the mess then blowing bubbles into it. Looking up he would say, "This stuff, it has the power of life, this is the power of life." And he would continue to blow into it. His mom called County Mental Health. They took him downtown but he was back in ninety days.

He came back with hair and a story about being Moses this time. He picked up the *Odyssey* and said, "I read this book. It's about a man, a man being chased. It's about a black man being chased by the bitch goddess. I know what is inside of every book. I have read every book. I am Moses, Black Moses."

One time I was in Bobby Cacaha's tattoo shop in Silverlake, Matt came in babbling with pupils gone total black, as if all the shit and sadness and insanity and toxicity had lodged in his eye and become his sight. He looked at me with a terrified smile, and walked up to me, but he could see that I was scared, freaked, looking like I saw a mad Matt. He wanted to cry, he was whacked out on something. He was tweaking and twisted, no shirt, no life that wanted to live, he got scared and ran, little and lost. He got put into a board and care soon after that. Then I didn't see him for a couple more months when he showed up at my apartment again.

I was working on another paper. This one about Neitzsche. I wasn't high. I had gotten to my own bottom, been too fucked up myself, too high, started thinking I was Johnny Future, man with divine plastic sauce sight. Started having my own raving cosmological tirades. Falling apart in school and myself. Now trying to put it back together and just graduate, just get over the line. I didn't know anything about Neitzsche. Only the idea that truth is much more severe and daunting than morality, it is, in fact, immoral. That is what I got out of Neitzsche. I got hungry and went to Zankou Chicken. I took Matt along. He ate up all the food. He was shaking. It was sad to watch him eat the chicken. His hands seemed so small and hesitating, like he didn't know what to do with food. What was in his mind? He knew he was insane. He had come to understand the world's prescription for his cracked sky of Black Gladiators. It was sad because he had known it all so well, his ideas, they were total, complex, detailed. He knew that heaven was a battling pearl with maggots and manna swimming inside its eyes. He just didn't know how to not know, too.

This is all bullshit. The fact is, he was sad, and he built up this hallucination to counter the pureness of his sorrow. In his life, his own life, there was nothing there, no people, no home, no him. His body knew no ground. We split for my house. And I could feel him, the weight of his perilous sorrow, heavy in the car. "Matt, I wish I could do something for you, but I can't. I can't give you what you need. You need some kind of heaven love to touch your sorrow. I don't have it. I don't know what can touch you." Thinking, the boy only needed a Jesus to come and touch him, he needed someone to blast his psychic veins clean of all the shit he had in him, but then what? Was he supposed to get a job? I always thought of that with him. What is he supposed to do to live? Can he ever get straight enough to deal with this shallow world and get a job where someone you don't like tells you what to do, yells at you if you don't, and can fire you if you don't like it? Where you walk around paranoid that something is gonna slip and you are gonna get the ax, like they might find out that you get high, or they might find out that you dig flowers, or are a communist, or that you don't like the shit you are making, or they might find someone who works harder than you, whose really into it and you're out, and you got to move? You have to be full of a certain amount of shit to work. Matt sat silently in the car and nodded. I don't know what he was nodding at.

Then I went to work on my paper and he went to sleep and we had some coffee in the morning. I never saw him again.

It was maybe a year and half, two years later and someone said, "Hey, you knew that kid Matt, Mateo?" "Yeah?" "He died." They didn't know how. They thought drugs. I did too. Somewhere I thought it was my fault. I was part of his bullshit, I found out later that he had a chemical imbalance, he took a lot of acid, smoked a lot of shit, but to me it was that boulevard speed that got him walking on water that wasn't there. It was just the push. After that time we got high, he said, "I ain't doing speed no more, too much animal pain in it." Then he was Jesus, then it was over.

Finally, I saw his mom on the bus, a born again this time, right here at Sanborn. I said, "I am sorry, I heard about Matt. It was drugs, right?" She said, "No, suicide. He jumped off the bridge right here. He killed himself." I am sorry, Mateo.

Some things in life seem so sad, sometimes life seems so sad, I don't know why or where its supposed to go, even with a family and a child and a child to come, I can't shake the fact, the knowledge that the deepest, truest and darkest thing is to be sad, tears are the fluid of our souls, we are nothing else but sad bones wanting to fall from our skins, sad skin, sad sight, sad light, living in sad times. There is nothing out there, no reasons, nothing to go to, this is it, the worst, the best, the hands, this is the deal, feel, know it, there is no revolution coming, there is no answer gonna be there for you, no music, no scene, no relationship, no life, no death, no nothing. What are we here for? I have believed those greater than myself, believed in what they knew, what they said, believed that there was something to it all, something like a god, or a light, or a devil, something that made you move, but right now, I don't know.

The streets look long right now. I decide to pull out my notebook and write something. When I get it out, there is nothing to write but that the streets look long right now.

I teach English right around the corner from here at Thomas Starr King Middle School. On the way to work, walking from the bus there is the occasional empty dong enlarger or butt plug package left on the curb. Dong enlarger, dildo, astro glyde and a butt plug, just right to top off the evening, intimate and pathetic garbage. It is the kind of garbage you look at and wonder how it got there and you imagine a car at 4 am and the guy with the dong enlarger pumpin' away in the front seat with some guy he does not know waiting, dabbing his asshole with K-Y. This garbage is deep and troubling because street fucking an anonymous someone with a dong enlarger that you bought from Circus of Books is a deep and troubled act. I pick the garbage up, I stuff it into the can. I am protecting the children, 'cause I know some freak punk kid

will smuggle the dong enlarger to school and chase girls
and boys waving the box with its Johnny Wad picture as if
it were his cock. Some kids see me throwing it away. "Hey,
Abee, what's that?" "Nothing."

Teaching English to 12 year olds in Silverlake, I cannot
believe that I do this. What am I doing? What the hell am
I doing here? I'll be standing in front of the class, and I
step out of my body, I sit down and watch myself, I sit
there and watch this guy give instructions, saying stuff
like, "Get out your homework," something like, "sit down
or I am going to call your home," crazy things, things that
no sane person would say to people, to kids, no sane person would do this to kids, would do this to themselves,
stand in front of a class and be authority, be Homework
Man, be Right and Wrong Answer Man, Mr. Red in The
Face, with my vein popping out, be Mr. Referral, be Mr.
Gives a Shit about how you act, what you learn, where you
are going in your life, Mr. Do Something with Your Life,
Mr. Open Your Mind, there is more to your mind and
heart than disco eye gloss tag banging trouble making, yes,
you are diamonds, luscious blood alive. I see myself and
laugh at him, Mr. Abee, he knows nothing, the fool, don't
believe him students, he does not care about roll call or
tardy sweeps, or even sentence structure. This Mr. Abee is
a funny man, he is troubled by a world of violence and
suicide, he takes great joy in ridiculous things, he wants
only warm sun, beneath a tree. He is out of his mind.

So I am a teacher. It isn't laid back, it isn't cool, it isn't
stoned. It is square baby, as square as the box the pizza
comes in. Kids should be running around outside, going
crazy in the pastures and jumping up and down in the

mud, they should be making naked lady pictures in the sky, they should be freaking out. There should be sex class, where the kids get to learn everything about sex and make all the stupid sex jokes and dick jokes and write down all the crazy dreams they have, make weird porn video projects using play dough for the actors, they should have mindless violence class where the kids just get to beat the shit out of things and maybe even each other. Oh, the blood would be too much, they could torture rats and things, that would get them ready for a career, any career, they could devise ways of killing, they could plan mass suicides and genocide, just get it all out, write it down, express their dark freaky kill visions, where everyone dies with a baseball bat up their ass, maybe this should be an elective. School should have a class where they get to really understand themselves, name calling class, fag hating class, parent hating class, teacher burning, maybe then they would stand a chance, maybe then they would be healthy. As it is now, they stalk each other in the bathrooms, they hunt each other in the locker rooms, as it is they deny any feeling that comes up in anyone, playing out the same frustrated and denial ridden pantomimes that their parents play, that the world plays, where people get hurt for real, freak for real because nothing that they are is understood by them, hatreds, hurts, desires, lusts, cruelty, love, they should have a love class where they have to pick flowers and love things and make sculptures and act out their loony love fantasies, write about things they love and things that make them sad, they should have sad class and deal with all the things they want to cry about, get it out, find out who they are, so they don't have to live with

these things popping out of their eyes and pores and ori-
fai, destroying them with strangeness, destroying them
with fear, with guilt and misunderstanding.

I need classes like this, but that doesn't happen, what
happens is the kids hate, and burn with hatred, some more
than others, some are nice about the hatred, they only hate
themselves, have no future idea of their life, or they are
nice as little kids then the boiling shit bubbles up into their
hands and they start freaking out. One year a little Disney
lover, wanting to please the parents, the next: a could give
a shit fail, their bodies like open cans of life that you open
for them and you love them, and you can't stand them,
you are a zombie after the day is over, you throw them out
of class, demand they respect you, when they don't even
know what that means. No one has ever respected them,
life doesn't respect them, no one listens, no one knows
them. How can they respect you? Failure is in them. It is
deep, thick like malignant nacho cheese they get for lunch
on Thursday. They accept it. It is the only thing that is
real. College ain't real. Kindness, something on public
television. And school is another world, a million miles
from home, books in a different language, parents can't
help them if they want, kids on their own from day one,
kids who are sharp, but got no words to put it together, to
get it out and into the world.

So what am I doing with my full-of-rage and insecure
ass standing in front of them? I don't know what I am
doing, I'm paying the rent, feeding my kids, trying to make
people think, all I want is a head full of butterfly skies,
things that don't frighten me and here I am standing in
front of kids who are told to look for strength in the

agents of empty death. They all see the bangers and the dying ones all over the place. They see them, they want to be them. Why not? The firemen don't put out the fires they feel, lawyers don't know anything about the laws that they know, these kids don't even know what they know, they don't even know that they need to know.

Fuck success, fuck making the kids think. Why do they need to think, think and become a person who is not easy to keep down, a person who wants something real in their life, who can't wake up for a stupid job, who will expect that there is something to life, who will get sad and insane when they see the only future is that of a drone, of a laborer in the mind of the machine? Can the world handle a bunch of Mexicans and Filipinos, or anyone of any color or kind who wants to destroy the game? Who wants the love real life style? Not the TV version, not the cereal box with a poster inside, not a Barbie car set on automatic pilot for the sunset of suburban righteousness. Fuck success. Fuck making kids think, making them ready for something that the world will never let them have. Why do they want to become people with open minds, people who think and want and need more than this world can deliver or allow? Who the hell let me into this gig? Who put me up here? There should be a law against this. There is a law, and those who have not broken it are the sick ones. Funny... I am good at this job.

The bus moves onto Santa Monica Boulevard. Santa Monica Boulevard is Grease Auto Part land, Special flowers, stoves and refrigerators on the sidewalk, greasy love secrets, radiator hoses and mufflers hanging like sausages,

poultry, guts and gizzards, telephone poles down to forever and the ocean is out there, yes and my car. There it is.
Jay's Jay Burger, the little shack, a monument of some sort
really, I think, no, I feel all the hamburgers that I have
enjoyed there, in the car or in the chair, with Penelope, my
daughter, when she was littler and the only child we had,
not all that long ago, sipping soda and saying "Ahhh" and
pointing to the airplane, the bus, the bird, and the night
club hoochie skirt wearing ladies walking with their kids to
the baby sitter on a Saturday night, or the drunkies laughing on the sidewalk, pushing each other and laughing
more, looking for a quarter that one of them dropped, but
woops, psych, "I got it right here. I never even dropped
it." Drunkies. The men behind the counter, they seen a lot
of drunkies, and I am gone on a dreamy recollection,
Double Jay, Double Jay, sitting in the summer breeze,
Cathy staring at me, bougainvillaea wraps around my
mind, I let go of the wheel and just eat the chili on the
inside, Steely Dan, Isley Brother's vibrations in my hair,
hipster damage walking worry eyed to the Garage, a club
that I've never been to. The little shack of burger, ply-
wood sides, a big wolf wind could take it away, but it does-
n't, it hasn't, it is here, as old as weeds. It has a row of potted cactus on its roof, inspires dreamy burger eating. And
I dream of the wind as it comes like it does out here in
Los Angeles, summer time. I look at the hills of Silverlake,
the palm tree line, the line of palm trees leaning back into
the star or two that is in the sky, the airplane winking, the
whole plane is dreaming of a Jay Burger, even if they
don't know what a Jay Burger is. I know they are, and all
the sleepy rooftops, ramshackle corrugated chicken coop

back yard dusty dusted heads and houses that I see and smell the jasmine breathed world and Penelope says, "Ma," which means "more," and so she sips some soda, but we are all up late tonight, maybe a drive to the airport to watch a plane land, or take off, to talk to each other as the streets go by and the dreams, dreamy dream dreaming dreamt deep desirous sirenous, eyes of all the eyes pass by, us passing by and we all know what each other is thinking on such a night, Eat at Jay's, Eat at Jay's, it has not blown away, I am hungry and back on the bus and the bus passes by, motorcycle cop, cinder block, log cabin, flock of seagulls on the top of the Las Vegas billboard, we all know what each other are thinking on such a day.

Wyatt Earp lived on Alvarado, at the end of his life. Did he live in a shack, old man western warrior? Did he die a destitute drunkard at the Mohawk bar, smelly whiskers, bent walk and as forgotten as the white washed weekday smoggy sunlight at noon? Empty sidewalk, empty sky, empty street, empty like only Los Angeles can be empty. Walking to the liquor store, loose change in his shoe, keeping him company, his gun long gone and sight gone too, and the sky skids out of view, killer of men, holder of justice, hero of folklore and film... would he drink his whiskey slow and wonder with the lemon moon, "If I had a nickel for every bullet, I'd be... (he thinks, looks out the window of his walk up wood shack, down at the traffic, a pretty young Mexican girl walks by)... happy."

The shacks of tires and auto repairs, seafood shacks, oysters on the half shell, restless decks of cards and bottles of the recycled, the shacks of paint cans and garden tools, the shacks of rust and weather, the ICE shack down Alvarado, with those cool chilled ice-cycle letters next to the Hollywood freeway, cardboard bum shacks, down in the tall bamboo off Temple.

Shack is the natural architectural form of this region, it is the house, the humble house that the angel's built saying, "Come and weep away all sense of time inside my lonely lonesomeness," lovely as the Santa Ana wind that rattles the wood planks apart. Yes, you can hear time coming apart in these little dry World War II bungalows, people suffering some kind of agrarian workers life in these little shacks of truth. Drinking, singing, shacking. Where are these places? I can't say.

They come into your sight like moths to light and then they are gone, buried in dandelion fields of memory, where the city has been forgotten and the earth let run up the walls: that is where these shacks exist, where someone needed a place to sell bird seed or sheep skin seat covers fast, they are burger joints, Taco Huts, the coffee wagon, Charlie Chaplin's film, *The Kid*, midnight flowers hanging desolate heads of beauty petals all along the cinder swept ground of love and limb and longing and lazy and learn the secrets of the smoke that embraces your eye in tear drops, crying, but you don't know why (that flower stand is down at Normandie, and only open till ten). The shack is a delicate structure. It is Los Angeles. Jimmy-rigged and sure for eternity. Go on Jay's Jay Burger and Hot Dog too, Auto Parts, no name closed window, Tires, WE HAVE MOVED, Union Swap Meet, aisle like a Byzantium Bazaar selling cumbia cassettes and stereo speakers, kitchen worker shoes, tube socks and deodorant shave cream.

Vermont Avenue

"*BER-MON*," CALLS THE BUS DRIVER. El Gran Burrito Restaurant is burning a skirt steak of cow on the half drum, carne asada, carnitas, bar-b-que smoke running over the roofs, good tacos, hard core tacos, I mean really Mexican, just the tortillas and the meat and you do the rest at the condiment bar with everyone else: the onions, cilantro, green chile, red, and you take a seat and eat at the benches, on the corner of the street, behind the black barred fence and look at the hand painted walls, big blue jobs with scenes from the fields of Michouacan, Zacatecas, wherever Mexico, rolling hills, cows, hail to the beef, a big thickly colored Virgen de Guadalupe looks down with compassion upon your meal of asada tacos with a radish on the side and the sign on the wall says in Spanish "we are not responsible for any harm that comes to you on these premises." The Virgen looks more compassionately at you, which makes the next bite taste just a little better.

Oh, Vermont Ave., oily gasoline ground, street I lived on at Kingswell, a denizen I was of the Onyx Cafe, oh, bohemian heart blood of the angel, unslick art making madsters, conspiracy theory ding dongs, "One Love" stoner kids close to God and full of shit and jazz, the lost ones, and there it was, hang of Beck, the loser who would be king, hang of Fulton Hodges, pages and pages written by the clear rambling lobotomy man. Who was that lady,

the one armed Scientologist, writing letters to L. Ron in a
Pall Mall insomniac stupor? The beat winos, broken crack
head Sweet P and Dennis, the genius, a chess man but just
mind gone, and murderer bums on the run, but I didn't
know that when I was talking to them, cause I was young
and dreaming everything into a poem, which it is, but we
just don't know how it goes… cigarette smoking, coffee
drinking, poem loving, napkin scrawling, hanging out for
hours, with all the sketchbook freakazoids and bent headed doers. What a place! Shit talking, dog allowing, free lat-
tes for pretty much everyone I knew, a great place to do
nothing and think about it, sweet strange island in the all
night empty city, serious—open to 3am, week nights,
while the rest of the city suffered, Vermont bus driver
would come in and say "there's messed up people out
there and I have got to pick them up." You would be
screaming and chirping with your friends, talking about all
kinds of sauce and then step out onto the street and see
what an island it was, 'cause nothing else was open on that
curb and no one else was out, someone would always be
there, ready to get right, to be wrong. That place was good
to me, even if the girl I went out with for three years
fucked me over in the end. I had it coming, it was coming.
I met Cathy at the Onyx Echo Park cafe, it was a nice
place to come down. Now it's gone, now it's gone. Go to
cool angels and smoke one in the tomb of gone away.
John Leech, you get free meals and drink for the rest of
your life in the place Cat and I will open one day.

Looka that—Vermont Avenue, always a vision from
some other world, the street of flames in 1992, the
Rodney King riots, the huge avenue, sick with flames it

was, insane all over, the city's pain and fear and hurt spilled arson tears all up and down its long avenues, this here Payless Shoes burned to the ground but was back before the second trial was through, other places, the empty lots still stand. I was in my apartment, with a view of the smoke and the gunshots ringing Lebanon Kosovo Koreatown Compton sweatshop rage in the blue sky, it was a nice spring day, it wasn't hot like people say, and I was sitting there writing the liner notes to my *Jerusalem Donuts* CD, thinking, this is funny, what does it mean? The fires felt like they coulda burned forever, everyone knew the hurt was deep enough, the freeways were full of apocalyptic panic, everyone knew, you bet, but it was all burned out by the next day. I was bummed out. I was freaked out by the rage and chaos but I was sad to see it stop for some reason. It was pure and true. The world was saying something that meant something. The plastic stupid sauce wasn't there. But it was over by Friday, and suddenly the city cared about its poor people, and it was mad at them for burning down the liquor store on their corner, people in Sherman Oaks were upset that Guatemalans looted in Pico Union when two days before, Pico Union didn't even exist… and now, it doesn't again.

Vermont is a spaced-out street. It is a place you write a postcard from and send it to Seoul, South Korea, and tell your brother to come over and get his. It is a street most fully gone *Blade Runner*. Is there a street like it anywhere in the world? Can there be? I say no, no and no again. There is no street like the street that I have seen in the naked rain of 3am, in my Plymouth Scamp, water through the roof, mind through the ceiling, loneliness I could make out with riding next to me in the car. No, not like then. No, not like I have seen it with sleepy headed driving sleep, on the way back from my sister-in-law's house, on the way back to our abode in Echo Park. We usually come down Olympic from Fairfax and come up Vermont and this is what I see: Olympic, just some cars, a few people on the street, the Korean walls are skies with fat letters from an alphabet that comes from alphabet trees on the other side of the sea.

Vermont Avenue, street of fires, street of Pollo Loco, long street, stretching all the way down to the South City sea of San Pedro, street that flows up into the chaparral hills, ending, twist and curve on the Observatory, green stained bronze dome on 1000 foot high hill top, where me and my friend Danny Wize, who bailed to NYC, we drove there in the 1990 El Niño rain, looking out on the city as it was roofed by caressing fields of rain clouds, just to drive through the Malibu light forest of Los Feliz and see like Maxfield Parrish in the Babylon rain. Did we feel the ghosts of the great DeMille and his celluloid chariots of Torah? I believe so, but it is hard to be sure, just driving and smoking, divining the breasts of the divine.

The dome of the planetarium was breast-like, sucked by a deeply clouded and stormed sky and the grainy orange lights of the city moaned a halo around the dome and the sky was Kabbalah with wheels inside the stars, celestine worlds in the notes of rain, mystic headlights bouncing through the fog. We stopped and walked, in something electric, and stood by the bathroom wall, listening to the voice of someone crying down the pipes into the sea, through all the drains, through all the pores.

Vermont Avenue, you laid your belly down, snakeskin of voltaic chemical circuitry, director of vehicular reason, directing our passing through many a life, you holding so many of us together with your concrete genius, idiocy, masterfully mute and rattling with sirens at the same time.

Vermont Avenue, Normandie Avenue, Western Avenue, each as long as the other, the three sisters, a constellation of urbanity, each stretching 20 miles down to the horizon of Anaheim street ARCO torches, Wilmington refineries, harbors full of cargo from all over the world, ships lumbering through the water, filling, emptying, and the harbor opens up into the sea, and the sea never forgets, the sea is everything. Vermont Avenue, Washington DC, Gaza, Tibet, Sri Lanka... shiny asphalt teeth filled with bits of sea, splendid street, darkest street.

Oh, tourist, do not come here thinking of La Reforma, or the Champs Elysee, whatever the fat street in Cairo is called, or Madison Avenue, or anywhere, not Market, not Beale, Lexington or Hollywood... all great streets, yes, but don't think of them here. See this only as it is: empty buildings, a vacant lot, a burger stand, and then a stretch of neon super malls, like ships of light, like vessels of luna sueños of the future beneath shimmering sparks of magnetized air, walls of Korean letters lit, pool room, soup houses, barber shops, discos and Hostess Bars, Karaoke clubs. This is the next world pleasure paradise of Korean Rolex decadence, BMWs and Mercedes Benz, 9mm, shotgun, and poverty of the undocumented slave all around. K-town golf ranges situated in the midst of 3rd world poverty graffiti scarred walls menacing the night with their promises of shotguns and forgotten ones, it is sad and it is wonderful and it is wonderful and it is sad and my moon swallows both pills along the slumber yard sea, because the streets of Korea Town are full of people from El Salvador and old ladies from the mid-west of America and there are other people too, of course, and cocaine sellers and people who have nothing but death on the mind.

Yes, but I have felt the breath of angels in the pools of orange streetlights that lay on the two block long streets, the really small streets, where some grandmas live with special candy and driveways full of roller skating memories and kids play and young lovers love and life is life no matter where you are, yes I saw this, not long ago, from the back seat, driving Reggie home with Dennis and Annette after a poetry reading in Venice. I saw stucco, dignified with its long cigarette ash on the carpet and dishes in the sink and the smell of old photographs and this is how I know this city, pearly-minded drives through the blocks and blocks of invisible forever.

I know these streets. I feel them in my feet, in my bones, in my toes, in my nos and yesses, in places I have not been, in my feet again, I feel this city stones and sea and desert and blessing and grace and disease and fear and hurt and addiction and corruption and endless bouts of sodomized hope, feel its rape and love and birth and death, its open wound, next door neighbors beating each other's ass all the time, for fun, old man, young man, bullets through the wall, mom and dad having midnight sex on the kitchen table, the table breaks, the movie ends, the kid wakes up on his homework, in the kicking mind of yellow nameless flowers across the sky. I am this city, my skin is the map, pimples, streetlights and liquor stores, stomach aches, and well that is just what you get when your eyes are Oki Dog big and strange.

I recall, right now, the day a few summers ago, when we, my wife, Cat, Penelope, our first daughter, and I... me, dad... we were driving back from the beach and took a slow day Pico Blvd. all the way into downtown and Suhiro Udon Noodle House in Little Tokyo. We floated down Pico, past all the queen dandelion blue walls of embryo's coming unglued from the freeway lily wind, past beauty girls, and pensive guys, past concerned eyes, open windows and empty pupusa cafes, baseball caps and aprons on a nail, the man, the cook, looking out the window, he was just staring at the fish in the moon too. Pico is a nude body in bed street, a cosmos of a street, it is an old street, like it is the way the horses went. The orbits of stellar bodies, gravitational pulls, the city spreads weird sisters over the ceremonial cauldron, faces from the world appear in the doorways, faces from other lands, faces of this land, and you are pulled apart by a glance, a look... I am the ragged palm tree whispering in tall-headed rows.

The streets all stretched with beauty mist blue smoke orange misted fingers and lips, moments of light passing takes root in your eyes forever. I wanted to cry, the streets broke my soul so wide open on this particular drive, and the people laid their lives inside my heart. I realized in a way I did not before, that we are all connected, regardless, no matter hatred, no matter love, no matter our matter we are all connected, cut out dolls stuck to the same surface, marshmallows in the same Jell-O, bones from the same tree, blood from the same river, on a street of dog lawns and domino porches, the shadows at the end of the street jumped into the prints of my fingers, smiling, crying, writing something in my intestines, gasoline butterflies the size of pin heads fluttering down park streets that lay somewhere before names and dimes. I could not take you there and say, "See." It was all my eyes and the slow hand of the sun as it said goodbye to this land that it had just spent so much time over.

Think about it. Having just dragged ass over this whole slab of earth, America and all that that means, evil soil, dirt filled with the ground down meal of dead nations, America, full of so many beautiful and sad dead things, filled with muddy sorrow and torment, America, long in muscle, hard in penis, sweet in sex and promise, bright in gamblers lamp light, deep in confusion, filled with ID cards and credit and full of life in plastic cups, full of death in plastic cups, full, never really empty, full in emptiness, never really full, full in deceit, in murder, full in another's land, in another's history, full in my history, one birth of a nation was the death of many others—500 years has brought us to this coast—that is the full story, this land, theatre of the greatest and most horrible societal crash and burn that the sun has known. Peoples moving as if they were continents with tectonic missions, to split and then converge again, to crash into each other and writhe up into something Himalayan. We, on this land, are part of something huge, a movement that only some great eye of being and death will be able to comprehend, and the sun has just laid hands over all of it, having brought the continent to life and now leaving, going away, to shine on the green scales of water, sunrise kingdoms to Asia, so in its final moments, don't you think that its sunlight lingers in an exhausted broom at the corner of the market, the little liquor store market that the old grandma runs, her granddaughter missing school to work stocking beer in the ice box, don't you think that after a whole continent of mercy and madness, of fat people eating Frito's cornchips, of murder and betrayal, of high finance, the sun stops, for just a single smoke at the last chance gas of this continental mind, an intoxicated man sitting in a folding chair calling out the time, he is a conductor on a stopped train, waiting for the northbound Starlight to pass on the tracks. Yes, the sun waits, mumbles wisdom, wants you to hear, but doesn't care if you do, you'll figure it out, eventually.

My mother lived on Vermont Avenue in the 40s. She lived right here at Vermont and Lockwood, then moved out to Rosemead, then back to LA, to 89th Street and Vermont, South Los Angeles. They call it South Central now. She drove my brother and me by the old house but it had been condemned. A lot of the area had. She and her family were part of the white flight of the 1950s. Orange County opened up and you could get a tract house with no down payment, so they moved to Buena Park, left South Los Angeles and she ended up working summers at Knott's Berry Farm and Disneyland. She was a can-can dancer in Knott's Berry Farm's old west saloons, a crucial role in the myth of Southern California. I have always been really proud of that.

I think of her, young dreamer of beatnik dreams in young 1950s Buena Park, Orange County, at the public library, a small building, stucco, one story, in the middle of a new tract and next to a strawberry field, and she put on the head phones, put the needle to the record. Her mind, what did it do? It was the MJQ, The Modern Jazz Quartet, she said something opened in her, something new, there was a place to go, a place that was bigger, smarter, a place for pain and anger and beauty. At 17 she had seen her alcoholic father dead at 42. Her entire life was lived hostage to her father's drunken rages and then he dies. No last talks. Nothing made clear or seemed better. Nothing said. Her mother was too scared to do anything herself, maybe pretending it all wasn't there, her little brother, just a little kid, quiet and burning ages in his own mind.

She heard the Modern Jazz Quartet and wanted to be a beatnik, more than that she wanted the cool that cooled the rage of the very air she breathed, the cool that came with the fluid vibes of Milt Jackson and the Piano of John Lewis, a sound that seduced the whole sad sky, why not? What else was she going to be? It was almost 1960. Everyone was aching under the yoke of straight corporate and clean progress, building bombshelters beneath their bar-b-ques, keeping yourself hidden, something had to give, and go beyond the searchlights. Did she get there? What is there?

She married my dad, the great Ralph Abee, a tidal wave of a man, an earthquake, an assault, a terrorist act, a genocide... the man is heavy. The world is a footnote to his tragic quest for the true illusions, anxiety and nightmares. Oh, don't get it wrong, my mother has a fireball in her eye, pissed off, full of love and hate, color spilling from her hands. They had a good time, they got down, they did cool stuff, driving up the Big Sur coast, getting magic bottles of vino at some middle of nowhere winery, making love in wine spilt tall grass. They got it on, bar-b-ques at the Monterey ocean, hitting the Monterey Jazz festival, it was good. They were trying to make a life full of love and meaning that maybe no world had seen before. It was good to be their kid. I feel special. They turned me on. I liked their crazy deal.

My father lived at Vermont and 3rd street when he came to Los Angeles in the fifties. He was 14 and moved into the heart of a young post World War II boom city that was already forgetting itself. Destitute streets, vagrant and alcoholic and dangerous and he lived at Vermont and 3rd where his father, Roscoe, was building a church. The First Church of the Nazarene, which is there, right next to Vons on 3rd street. The streets belonged to the Temple Street Gangsters, TST, who are still around. They practiced a version of their brutality on him and his Portland, Oregon, ways.

His parents and sister lived in a little trailer on the construction sight and he lived in an army surplus tent set up out by the street. He learned the fear of the city and it never left him. Frankly, I don't know how he survived. I don't know how either of my parents survived. My mom I could see buoyed by the new suburban life at the right time in her life, even though her home life was insane, but my old man, I don't get it. I don't know what dreamy angel opened its wings to him but one surely did.

I am crazy from growing up with them. They made me. The Existential Lawyer soaked in the blood of the Lamb and the Mad as Hell Disneyland Tour Guide with the soul of art pouring out of her fingers. I love the crazy shit inside of me. I am happy my parents were insane and unhappy, that they couldn't stand there lives, that they were freaking out for something more, more money, more love, more drink, more Jesus, more Jazz, better kids, a better apartment, a better job, more and more better. I am overjoyed that they screamed about the life they lived. I am happy they did crazy shit, breaking stuff. Fuck, I wouldn't have had it any other way. I am happy my folks got all jazz nasty crazy drunk punching out the years of their life. I am happy that I think love must hurt and that I know life will break you. I am happy that I don't know what happiness means. I am happy that I know, no matter how crazy you are, if you got some kind of love in you, you are gonna be some kind of alright.

Red head white guy madman, a box of radio parts that he keeps leaning over and playing with, tuning something, mumbling "Goddamn it, can't hear, too many people talking," and then he puts his head back down and tries to listen but nothing… The old Mexican woman sitting next to him, looks into his box with curiosity, then looks at him, he looks at her and says "I can't hear anything, it's too loud." She nods and smiles. The madman gives up and pulls out a beat up newspaper and tries to read, someone moving down the aisle steps on his foot.

Marouch, Arax Bakery, old men playing that game they play on the porch, they play forever, Armenia for Life, Cadillacs bump to Lebanese-Armenian disco sirens as they tool down Mariposa, the old women nod from the porch just back from a walk to the store, arm in arm, gray brush-like hair and stained teeth, staring at the sun, waiting for it to make a move. They are Old World in the land of sun and destruction, Los Angeles and the New World future and all that hysteria, the only Old World I've ever seen really live here. A people who stay a people at any cost, surviving genocide and diaspora, assimilation and just being forgotten, they know themselves, a culture going back 3,000 years. Man, do they piss people off. Like where I work, at school, 9 times in 10, if they have to pick groups for something it's always with other Armenians. They really love each other. How can it be that way? Why weren't they part of the cultural landbreak/annihilation that was, that is America, that is Los Angeles? How have they survived? The old women cut you off in any line, market, bus stop, carwash, and look you in the eye and not smile or blink or care, and the macho guys are a pain in the ass when they are standing around laughing at you and your shoes, running you over with a Mercedes full of food stamps… it's America, Los Angeles, I wouldn't want it any other way.

And I see her in dust swirling across a parking lot, on Mariposa, Nuestra Señora, the queen de Los Angeles, in the desert there is a woman waiting for a ride, to the coast, if you pick her up you will never be on the main road again: DETOUR. She's bad, she's broken, she's a high plains healer who never ends what she begins, she's a vixen with a shark fin tattoo. She is a seamstress queen that spins sails for your lunar tide, woman city of dust, in the dirt along the sidewalk, in the mangy critters of the curb. "This city is a woman," Cathy said to me as we were driving on the freeway, one sunset, past downtown. "The earth here is female." What does that mean? A blind blooded woman river, some golden womb of sea, a woman on the desert moving to drown in the ocean, one who bleeds pulse lines and tear drops of the extreme, all the extremes, from nothing to no one to all the world and back into all the directions of the in-between. She lays on this bus. Drunk on candy wine. Speaking a mile a minute, real soft, gum stain rain. This city, this angel, is so alone. She is not like the rest of the land she is attached to. This is where the Greyhound stops. This is the nether land. This is far away. This is where the land ends. What can phallic America understand about her solitude?

Los Angeles, I must be honest, you are horrible, really an insane place, I don't know why I love being here. I must be insane, I must be a fool, you have trapped me, trapped me with your meaninglessness, a prison of empty skies and long eyed nights, your big fat streets full of cars and frantic billboards, sidewalks full of vomiting men and lost immigrants, and no one wants to be here, no one wants to be from here, no one thinks of here when they are here, they all have come here for the money, for the stars, to get a new car, to change their hair color, to do all manner of cosmetic improvement, but who is here, really here, who loves the sun, besides me?

It is a lonely place, it is loneliness that brought people here, it is loneliness that dots the sky bright in the sunset hour, fills the streets with nothing, drives people out, cursed ground, filled with the blood of nations raped and destroyed, what did you expect? City of morons, meat head mayors, uptight preachers, myopic vein popping big-

ots of every race and flavor, street corner vendors of
doom, hip losers looking for a last chance, and all of this
is really why I love this place, because it is so error ridden,
because it is so lost dog on the edge of the world, it is all
talk, the Colossus of Confusion, it is driven by something
that it can't control, it is rage in sunlit stalks of sugar, it is
people, living nowhere, nothing sure, no one believing in
the center beyond themselves, just them and their car, or
them and their bus stop or them and their hair, no one
buying the American dime, no one looking around and
seeing anything that means more than what they know. It's
a good city for a mechanic... lotsa cars.

I am crowded on the bus, a man is sitting next to me. He
is taking up too much space. He doesn't know this. How
can he not know this? How can he sit there, leaning all
over me? And I'm trying to give him enough room, but
he's just leaning further, all over me. I don't mind the contact, it's not that. Contact, whatever, I'm on the bus. It's
what I expect, but this is not cool, this is not funny, this is
why wars start and bad blood comes up to your ears, people don't give you what you need: room to sit, a bite to eat.
   I sit squashing myself against the wall, and I know that
he can feel me. I look out the window, I look down the
aisle. Who cares? So what, I am squashed. I am small, getting smaller. I am nothing. This man cannot sense the
needs of my humanity, because I have none, I am nothing, I am larva waiting to hatch. I am the car that ran out
of gas and was left on the side of the freeway. Yes, you
have seen me, that's who I am, gnat tiny dog empty piss
can. I love this man with a mustache and booze wild eyes,

booze and ass-kicking. Looks like he gets into it, and he doesn't really care where or when. So I sit squashed and I know it is because, in his weird way, he wants me to know that he is there. Yes, he wants me to know that he is in the seat. I feel good. I feel that I have responded to his need for dignity. I am a good citizen. I am pleased with myself. I shake my hand. I give myself the key to the city. He moves a little, gives me some room.

This woman sitting with her hands in her lap, right across from me, she is sad, as sad as the shades of rivers, the ghosts who died of broken hearts, who left cold windows alone, in grief that you can feel with a glance, she sits with plastic bags full of things from some store, some place, she went to buy toothpaste, mouthwash, aspirin. These are the things you buy if you are sad. Her eyes well up like rivers, smell like days without anything to eat. The tears have made trains down her spine and teams down her belly. I look at her and I wonder what has made her weep so, has she seen too many of her children die to look at light and not cry? Who has left her with her wounds full of mouths, and her mouth full of ashes? The day grinds her down, down to the bones, one bone at a time. Is that milk she is carrying home? She looks up and she sees nothing and looks away and looks down the aisle, looking out into the street, where the trees wag their hungry heads up out of the sidewalk.

A man in blue work shirt and dark blue work pants, a mechanic, a painter of cars, a plumber of pipes, he stands in the middle of the aisle, holding onto the bar over head, swaying with the traffic, watching cars. He sees a woman outside the bus, she walks with her head down. She has lovely breasts. He nods to her. She looks like something he may have dreamed, he wonders about names, looks at his hands, picks his finger, a scab falls to the floor. He checks his back pocket, his wallet, it's still there. And then he doesn't look like he is thinking about anything, he looks like he thinks that he is the only one on the bus... amazing, in a way. It is lonely to be king.

A dog barks at a lady pushing kids in a shopping cart, the dog is behind the fence of the auto repair. The dog walks back and forth behind the fence. The dog smells carne asada, lifts up his nose. The dog barks, again and again. A boy throws a rock at the dog. The dog jumps into the fence and bites it. Looks up at the sky. Looks down on the ground. Cars and people and exhaust and busses move around him. He lays down to nap. He dreams of a fence with a big hole in it.

An old Mexican man, with Indian in his face, looks down at me and then away, a bit tripped to see a white guy right here, right now, I believe. He is just looking for a seat and I wonder what I look like to him. He is older, lived through the hardest times, when white society had laws against him, when there was a white society here. Now the only thing that the white world has left here are the sewer pipes and the bus lines. The billboards, they are in Spanish now. American Capitalism has embraced the immigrant Latinos as a market worthy of commercial exploitation. Welcome to Fantasy Island. Tide does not care about you or your clothes, just your money. Because here, in America, to sell is to be and to buy is to be American.

What does this man see? What do I see? What about

anyone? What do they see? White skin or brown skin or
black skin. The people that fucked you up. The kids who
beat you up and stole your stuff. Zoot Suit lynch mobs,
Storm Troopers, 3rd grade rapist, cop-faced teachers, riot
police, the lady who spit on you when you came back
from the war, the people who took your family's money
with a law, somehow something that no one understands,
or the bulldozer that put that man's house underground,
what does anyone see when they look out at the world and
its people?

This old man, he is calm. Has he surrendered to the
facts of a sad world, where some have and others do not,
where some beat and others get beaten, where the lawful
are not, where color means everything and where color
means nothing, because all have sinned and beaten and
been beat, somehow, or does he not care about anything
but his own, just those who warm his table and let him
into their hearts? The world changes more than he. Who
is stronger?

The man stands there as if looking up into the moon.
What is the moon? I think it is a jumping dog catching
mind in its teeth. How long has he been here, in Los
Estados, El Norte? Has he been to the Galleria? Walked
in, looking around, stopped right in front of hurried
shoppers. "Many people, much noise, but none seem to
be talking. How is that?" And he gets through the food
court and then he stands in the middle of the main esca-
lator with others moving all around him and sees the plastic ceilings and the walls of glass that house the cosmet-
ics, shoes and baseball hats. So many shoe stores. The
shoes make a man. And so he sits down with a smoothie

and watches his family disappear, "Meet you back here abuelo, at 5:00, American Time." And he sips his drink and waits.

All anyone wants is respect. I, Steve Abee, desire such. I desire kindness, become mad easily, am bitter, full of love, vicious when hurt, hurt easily, feel the world against me, feel naked, open, got no defense, must be right, a lot, can't stop the jeering wind, vulnerable as a pulpy mass of uterine blood wall held up to the rushing traffic. I don't know how I have lived this long, full of hatred, full of tears, buckets of the suckers, it is something I inherited, something that lives inside me with its reason coming from places and things I really do not understand, I don't know, I am American, and that is all I can say. Thelonious Cholo Mouse Disease, Grandfather Bushmill's Chevrolet Tombs, Jesus Towers of Apocalypse light, Lover, hold me up all night, ALCOHOLIC, DRUG ADDICT, FAN OF PORNO, father and husband, educator, WRITER OF DERANGED GOSSAMER LYRICS, DECIPHERER OF TEXTURES OF PRIMORDIAL BREATH GEMS MELTED IN A RAPID TRANSIT SUN, A HIGHLY MORAL MAN, ANARCHIST, BELIEVER IN NOTHING AND LOVER OF EVERY GOD THAT EVER WALKED ON LEAVES, INSANE, neurotic, SEER OF POETRY IN POOLS OF OILY RAIN WATER AND OLD LADY TOES IN LINE AT THE MARKET, got no gold, got no coin, got no marching orders, got no drum, got my hands and the hands of the one I love, everything I am comes from the night, an old man. I am an old man. I am American and you all on this bus are

American, everyone everywhere on this city grid, is American, even if you don't wanna be, you are, everything this country possess you possess, dog food cancer and castles of love, you must want it, you must demand it, it is our right, and it is this right that makes us insane because you cannot have what this country possesses. I will tell you a secret. You must become a nation of your own, make your own laws, your own rules, your own God, your own angels, your own people, America will kill you, otherwise. I am old man America piss drunk in the backyard, making dolls out of aluminum foil. You must be everything that America is not. That is the American way.

A kid rides a big wheel over a crack in the sidewalk, Hobart, Hollywood Star Lanes, with its spastic atom neon sign and blue stars on the inside walls, some great names have bowled perfect games there. Ben Hur Auto Mechanics is next door, a man with a hat on his head walks into the lanes, a drunk old man walks out. This is what the old man says: Fuckin' hot, sun in my eye, bus, goddamn bus in my way, wassa Pupusa? Pup Uh sa... hmmm, sure a good looking gal. Wish I was randy. Used to be a cocksure fella. What the hell? Still got a dog in my yard, goddamn day is over, what I do, went in for a drink, came out, come out, right now, day's gone. Beers felt nice. Good to drink a few, funny joke, how many drinks ya have? Oh, just one or two, or three or four. Been that way since 1946. You ever wonder how many goddamn burgers are cooking in this city? Millions, I bet. Sky reminds me of things. Looks like someone set a fire, some place. Better go back inside. Don't feel so good. Better call a cab.

Already called one. Gotta feed my animals. Sunset sure is pretty. Looks like a painting. Looks like a Japanese painting. Never seen one, but I bet it looks like that.

JON'S Market, Little San Salvador #2, the Tiki Room, Payless Shoes, we ain't moving too fast, the cheap stores full of plastic trucks and cheap hair gel, plastic lip liner poverty, the Hollywood Freeway full, taillights and exhaust, the freeway, conduit of the working bee, massive river bed of concrete, stretched out like something that doesn't belong. I want to say like an abstraction taken concrete shape and form, like an idea of a life, it is some kind of symbol, like the Pyramids, The Colossus, the Eiffel Tower, the beacon of a world, a huge bed of car lanes, telling eternity what this world believes, meant to stand in the hot sun, a testament, searchers of the future will know our mind by this structure, they will know, know what? That we believed in nothing? That it is all about getting to work and back home and that is it. That everyone fends for themselves. That we are bound in concrete and steel by alienation and freedom. What the hell does it say? Nothing, nothing at all, it's just a way to get some place. That's all.

Bukowski walks to the laundromat, a paper sack of clothes, a beer, and an orange in his bag.

My aunt Betty, well, my great aunt, my grandmother's aunt, she lived a few blocks from where we are, down on Lemon Grove and Serrano. I wonder if she ever saw the face of Chinaski. Probably made a funny face at him as he passed by. She told my mom before she moved: Lots of weird people in my neighborhood, Donna.

She went insane. Ended her life at a retirement home

in Hancock Park. She used to hallucinate that there was a man with a gun after her. It seems kind of funny, in the way that insanity is funny. There was a man after her. The rest of the world couldn't see it but it was there. She called the police. It was real. What was it? Fear that she never let out, pain and guilt and sorrow, coalesced into a stalking demon with a ski mask and a hunting rifle, eyes on her death? Poor old lady, demons on the balcony, pure America. America is a poor old lady with a troubled family, hallucinating demons on the balcony.

Poor old lady.

WESTERN AVENUE

MANY GET OFF THE BUS, and some get on. Western Avenue, a nerve line of the city, the street goes all the way down to San Pedro, furniture stores for miles, the avenue beautiful when lit, the lights of street life mania wiggling all the way into the horizon, people moving in all the directions that we have to go, dirty street, shoe store on every corner, El Salvador poverty, third world hustlers, keys made, Ritmo Latino, the black lite transvestite bar, nasty porno joints, a great and sketchy corner with El Pollo Loco once again and a Hollywood Video, too.

I lean against the window, the bent up guitar player stands outside the Botanica palm reader store. He doesn't have any strings anymore and how do you describe the eyes of the kid man with a permanently beat down eye, talking intensely to his buddy, leaning all over the sidewalk? There is a sun dried, street creased faced lady who looks gypsy with bangles and gold thread in her hair, wearing sunglasses and sitting quietly in the mayhem of everyone else's Western Avenue. Someone is snorting on this bus. And someone is making kissy noises. The sidewalk is full of people, man with a baby, baby with a bottle, woman in office skirt and painted nails, woman making mango change, CRAZY CUT KING DONUTS, Salvador hip guy selling cigarettes and fake IDs, honking cars and cashing checks and the ladies at the other bus stop, waiting to cross the street, the apartments with the

thin stoves of beans and grease on the walls, where someone new just came to town, needs a place to stay, he's a
cousin, he's a compadre's brother, he's family, give him
something to eat, so she puts down her heavy day and
makes him some consomme, her husband motions:
there's room for him on the floor, they need another guy
at the restaurant, we'll go down there tomorrow, and it's
all sad and that's okay. And there is the tired girl by the bus
stop, she waits for the bus down to 8th street, her family
won't return her calls… and then boom, madness, aaaaah-
hh, eeeeehhh, all these people explode, sadness, happiness, so whatness, explodes, oh my God style, flesh and
guts everywhere, the galactic marbles, the pieces of their
lives become butterfly wings of flesh up against the sky,
they are decapitated and one man, whose infidelity leaps
like a billboard from his head in the final moments of his
life, is castrated by the fiery shrapnel membrane of my
bus's body.

It is an orgy of violence, I scream out in horror, I am
killed in this explosion, the catastrophe has taken all of my
ribs and spread my intestines out over the dirty ficus trees
of Western Avenue, shoe store windows are filthy with my
fluids, blood dripping down at Sears and onto pupusa
joints. Oh, my Lord, it is horrible, it is disgusting, all is
lost, all is lost, I am seen for what I truly am, an animal, it
is long over due, people discover my remains. They say,
"He is strange. He seems to be bubbling. His skin is not
really skin but it looks like a film of soda with tadpoles in
it. No, that's not it. It is a house full of eyes. Yes, that is it.
A house of eyes." "I think he had a cancer. Look at his
bones. Yes, eaten up by life, eaten by the worms of the

day, his bones eaten away by the sun. Incredible, he doesn't exist except for this cancer of city, in fact, we cannot see him, he's not there, just bottle caps and condoms and unnameable filth." The end should have come sooner, but that is not possible… that is not so, the bomb explodes, we die with life spilling from us, such a horrible people, such ignorant fools, chasing the carrot, whatever the carrot may be, so not to be sung about or seen as anything but bricks. Abee, you sentimental fool, you idiot, naive, sophomoric at best, not punk at all, not hard not at all, what are you doing, where are you going with this bus? But that is THE WAY IT IS. Sorry, human beings=sentimental jewels. Deal with the spider arms of star fields and land mines in the eyes and pocked skin of the bus, deal with the intestine hanging bloody language all over the places where we make our lives, all our lives, pots and pans and hair spray on the shelf of the dollar store are covered with our tender flesh and vicious dreams. The explosion subsides, the dead are counted, bagged and shipped by the Lord and then get up and go on with their day.

The city of exile performs here at Western avenue, in this basin of angels, a nexus of worlds south and east and west, the dream direction for each culture that comes here, the dream within the dream of America, the dream of work and a new life for all our brothers from the South, the dream that no one believes but many follow just the same. The most American city, full with dream demon angel death freight, American because it is not America at all, this is the sand of strange shaped hours at the end of the line. It's no big thing. It just where the land stops and so America stops, what can you expect then but madness and killing, because when the dream does not come true, when the dream is your own spiritual and cultural suicide, then you must wage war with yourself at least. This is what I am doing here, I am murdering myself, it is the will of the people and I am creating something in my place, a new race, a nude race, a race of nude race car racers, nude creation is being done by the voices that surround me, that surround us, that surround time.

The cosmic dogsled race, the solar blue note cacophony spreads out space and wheels, rapid transit sacristy, cool notions in a hand bag held tight, the anatomy of the distance between my arm and the arm of the man next to me and the man next to him, we are the explosion of seeds, the anatomy of severe air breathed so quietly, invisible structure, answerless phones, shaping hands of gravity, spit, come and love. Our heads hang exploded in the heat of nothing, skulls like melons broken because there is nothing to stop us, God give us a rule, make us less than we are, make us more, make us.

Oh, Father, who art, be us better than ourselves, saliva seed sewn in the dust, magic hand of delirium coughing minstrels, maybe we better stay in tonight, God is gone, God is silent, God doesn't care, God gave the world what it wanted, he split, jettisoned the vehicle, the divine brain left long ago and we are as big as the night and as small as mud, free, totally and completely free stella explota daily donut cosmonautical skippers and Gilligans, the Professor and Mary Ann, but whose island is this, really?

There is a hole in the sky, where there is no difference, no is and isn't, no was and will be, where it is all water, inside and out, where there are no more names, we need no more names, we need the named, the thing, swing of love, wind kisses, wings of benefitia bone, to be vehicles of light, card carrying members of the celestine core, to decipher our shadow packages, pass out harmonicas made of sparrow bones putting forth tones only the tides know and then turn us out into the streets of ourselves to make music and sell our cotton candy love, it is all good.

String us up, take out our eyes and make us find them, search the floor, the ground, graveyards, the altars where the flesh is burned, search the ashes of parents, the bones of children, the ghost fog, the Jerusalem mist, the blue whale burial ground, search through the tombs of grocery clerk saints who did what they did only for the doing, search through the yellowed and brittle archives of calavera flowers, the libraries of veins, where nothing is written but is spilt, bloody and fungal, left on the ground, stains around a bus bench. Sit there, let the worms come to you, come kissing you, sucking you clean one hair at a time, let the microscopic kingdoms of skin bugs grow up into your brain, deteriorate with the kisses the stars brought to you on platters of spring, behold the nimbus about the dog that trots beneath the pawn shop marquee...

Wilton, thick with neon signs and Central American food joints advertised in bright red or yellow, mini-malls screaming spazmos of color, streets full of gum stain alphabets. Fat stinks, spirit of the living hot dog wrapped in bacon, beer upon the ground, a body of goodness, a body of badness, surrounding us, perfume, food left on the sidewalk, parking lot puke from the night before, gently mixed in, and then you leave but your smell is there and it talks to other smells, and they make new smells, and you can't see any of it happening but smell the cooking, of smells and say, "What's that smell?" It is you and Tom's or Ted or Fred's Liquor store love nest of wino sidewalk crawlers, Goldiggers bar on the street front of an apartment that houses families crowded into rooms where their lives spill out the windows, red carpets for curtains, and knick-knacks that come with a Big Mac and pictures of Jesus and Guadalupe, apartments that house the righteous sorrow of the poor.

I look at the ladies of the universe, that is what I call them, the women who go all day, week, life, long, to work in the rich houses. To clean someone else's life and not have time for your own. I knew a woman, she did this for the family of the girl I was dating, I have not seen the girl in many years but the lady I have seen more recently, on the bus, in fact.

All that aside, one day at the girl's house in Beverly Hills, a movie star Spanish style mini-mansion from the Twenties, in the land of wealth and impatient plastic surgeons in fast cars, I was in the backyard, throwing matches in the empty pool, it was hot, the old lady maid Yolanda was planting pansies and told me to come over. I did and she held up the flower and said, "This is reality. This grows in the ground." And she stroked the velvet petals and I don't remember what else she said, or what I said. But this I know right now: the only thing true and real is a flower growing, anything that is a flower growing, that is growing, that is IS and not NOT, that does not search out negation of others in order to be, does not determine value by grading against another, that simply glows with itself, that is no less than any other, that is no greater, that is the real thing, itself, and the quiet flower sits growing in somewhere earth, in somewhere eye, in somewhere hands, and it is little and its smallness is naked, fragility so loud you must stop the car, walk in a circle and listen, the fingers of its essence are wrapped around the sun and you see this flower, this moment, this flower moment cut out of time, no clock or calculation surrounds its being, it hums with its own universe orbiting black holes and sinking into luscious pots of truth, yes, yes, yes, she was a special woman telling me how the delicate things are the world and that their survival is the only truth that makes the world last. She wore thick glasses and spoke in lisping Colombian Spanish, and here we are, petals of sunlight streaming through us, here we are the moment of something larger than our clocks can count and moved by something much smaller than our dreams can breathe.

I don't really live here in the world. I get along. I get the bills paid on time but I live somewhere else. I live in the Avalon balloon, an atmospheric swimming pool. Really, I live with my wife and daughters, working hard to be warm in our little flower. The mind pollution freezes over our house and falls away, haha, this is what I really want to say, I am safe with my love and children. I need them because the world, I do not believe it. The world, it will not be this for long. This stuff, these hanging fences and twisted men, it will not last. It will end. It has ended right now. It has ended for human beings. This is what I am trying to get to right here—I am just preparing the car, mapping my part of the road, really my daughters, really they are the ones that are going to be involved in freaking the world real, whatever that means. I have already died, I have died for love and come up with them and my bones are smiling because really we are really in this life, against the death squads, against the death of mind and imagination squads. Fight that war or the other wars won't count. They don't. Worst thing is there will be no reason for a war, nothing to fight for.

I am dog tongue true and I am none of the above. I am misspelled nirvana. I am cough drop lolly pop for the old age teeth mart, spiritual french fries psychology dog shit super cap gun electrolux. I don't want anything, I don't care about this world, I don't give a shit about the real world, my world is real, I only care about my pretty ones, my wife and babies, sunflowers, yellow flowers, I am sipping with the love bees inside of my true love's brain. That is what I care about. I care about everything you can touch and feel. Everything that bleeds. Everything that flows. The flower that is. That is what I care about. That is reality, that is the source of the River Seine, the Nile, this is where the corn first grew, the egg from which the conquering eagle flew, the future is the devil with no eyes, it has propelled us into our heads and out of our minds and will take away the breath of our souls. Invest in biotechnology, it is coming, you might as well get rich off the replicants and collect all the analogue recordings that you can and open a library. The mistakes, the stink, the blossoms out of sync with time, the experience of self will be so hyper-mediated that we will find ourselves not knowing a real experience from a digitally crafted kiss. Thus, the revolutionaries will be gardeners, not toppling states, not killing cops, but living life as it is, being stronger than the fight the generals would have us be clowns in, not dying by their rules. No, we are living here, making life from seeds and eggs.

Hollywood Cemetery, a very special place: bleak cinder block wall around the block, stones at the gate like dracula castle stones, bent rows of tombstones, gothic angels and stone birds protecting the dead, here in Hollywood, the Hollywood of Santa Monica Blvd. and Gower Avenue. Hollywood of immigrant hunger, of American need, Hollywood of Mack Sennett and backyard orange blossom melancholy, crows flying over the graves, smoggy sunlight withering the wreaths, time trying to wipe the names off of the stones. I want to be buried here. Put that down some place. Either here or in my backyard amongst my paint can poems and trees. I hope I have a backyard when I die. I hope I die in the backyard and fall like tired fruit and rot into the ground. But if not that, then here, right next to Douglas Fairbanks' mossy tomb or by Mel Blanc and his thousand voices, or put me around Valentino and his lonely roses or by the victims of the LA Times bombing from 1912, a cynical frame up of the IWW, which kept Los Angeles a union-free, open city. Oh, city makers, why were you so afraid of the free? You have scarred us with your fear of human faces. Put me in the back, amongst the crowded and uneven stone rows of older graves, the names you can't read, or by the Armenian couple that lived across six decades and three continents with each other, who died within two months of each other, their faces carved into their grave stones.

The grandmother died first, her funeral procession came down the streets, old country style, walking to the grave-yard. The family walking, in black, weeping old tears. The procession came down Hobart to Fountain, to Wilton, to Santa Monica, where they were stopped by the police and given a ticket but allowed to continue on the sidewalk until here, where the priest, in orthodox hood, waved the incense over the grave, so that the spirit would know that the Lord was there. The incense holds onto the air, looks across the stones, wraps itself into the grass, the dead have flown and we the living are left with the perfume.

There is a display window to one side of the entrance with a sign over it that reads "Flowers" and at night the sign is lit, not neon but small clear round light bulbs. Ivy hangs around the word and the rest of the cemetery is dark, palm tree shadows and the iron gate. All you see in the entire world is the word FLOWERS. The light bulbs stir up something sepia, a smell of dried rose petals, dust, brittle yellow pages of a favorite book, long out of print, unknown, not literary, but in this picture, the one I am seeing, it is a grave book of memory and inspiration. It is full of sayings and stories that show you life is worth liv-ing, and life is sad, and life is happy. None of the lines are confusing. They are order to chaos, they are not much in themselves but become something when they reach into the eyes of the reader who savors them, leaves a flower on the page of the poem, the gravity is in the effect, in the act of the human being touched by something, no matter what, where the human heart flies to is the thing, where the wind came from is unknowable and finally inconse-quential, what is it that these people felt deeply in their burden of sunlight? Hollywood cemetery, rest in peace you merry man, oh, gentle woman, make glad with the sparrows that call your name in the middle of sea bottom dreams.

I go to cemeteries once in a while, haven't taken the kids to one yet, but the thing is I think about life there. The dead propel us to decorate our meat, to carve our voices into song, to mold the stone to fit the images of the eternal ocean that is in our mind, a cemetery refreshes you, you become aware of the texture and bend of your arm as it is brushed by the wind. The wind stops you, makes you touch your face, feel your name in your hand, the dead are so quiet and thoughtful and final that you are sure of life. You stand in the midst of the plane of being, the dead from a hundred years ago, the dead from ten years ago and you see the time in which they lived and died, feel the cut of sky they lived under, walking on the lawn they walked on, to the car they drove, to the stretch of the street that they lived on… how it looked with rickety little houses, nothing there, or not paved, not in a car, horses. And then you see the ground spread out from that place, where that body lay decomposing in the box, you see the rest of the world come down to this point, this place, everything comes to this plot, all arrows point here, and you feel that the whole earth is a grave, every scratch of earth and drop of wine holds the remains of the canals of mind and body that were this life for someone.

Burying dead people is ancient. An act of vision and faith, putting the dead body back into the earth that gave it birth, naming the space the body lived in, blessing the fire that has gone out, acts of faith and dreams as old as our eyes. Why do we do this? Will we always do this? What will it mean if we do not do this? What stopped that man, that woman and told them to dig a deep hole and put their dead child into it? It was grief, huh? Deep, bad, grief. They couldn't just leave the child to the dogs, to the flies. The child wasn't really dead. There had to be something else, somewhere, a place that the light in those eyes had gone to. There has to be. That was my child, that was my love and bone, not to be forgotten, to be alive is to be dead, and to know the dead, to love the dead, is to be alive.

But come on, God? Spirit? Forget it. Just flush the dead away, like crap, like trash, why mark their lives, what did they do? I mean you look at these people in the ground and feel so solemn about everything but who knows what these people were all about. Did they live hating niggers, or did they rape their sisters, did they steal from their own dying mother, did they masturbate on the curb, go to church and damn the poor and vote for a madman, maybe they thought Hitler was on the right track, or maybe they made little dioramas in their basement, painted portraits of angels that they saw in the trees, and no one ever saw the paintings, and they died alone, their house full of decaying garbage, rotting food in the corners of the rooms, dead animals in the kitchen, and them finally dead, for months before someone came by Why do we mark the lives lived, people we didn't care about, the souls that we don't know, that we bury then let go, that are never visited? I'll tell you why. If we don't we will be more fucked that you can ever imagine. If you don't love your dead, you can't love the living and hell, life is short and the work and worry and struggle and pain doesn't add up to anything unless we say so.

Death, you are frightening and sad, I don't care what anyone says. Faced with your own end or the end of someone you love, only a dead person would feel no fear. Fear of so much sorrow, loss, new world, gone world, life without love near, without their life and the recipes for canning peaches that they had. Sacred end, common port-hole, toward what, who, where will we go, why go, what was the use of doing all this, then? I can't see past you, Mr. Dead. You're blocking my vision. I will die, you will die, my father will die, almost died last year, how will it be? My mother will die, my wife will die, oh lord, what will I be? My children will die, how can that be? They were just born. You are wicked. Do you get sad when you do what you have to? Some poets think you do. Stay away from my friend. He just had a baby. How is it going to come to me? How will I die? What will I see? Where will I go, two min-utes from now, a year from now, ten years, in a car, or on the street, in my sleep, or old and in the sun with a fly landing on my purple tongue? I want a piece of buttered toast in my hand when I go. I want to be thinking of some pretty things. You hang in the air, Sir, Lady, I cannot tell, you are no clown. You sit, as calm as light, in the seat right in front of me...

Blank stucco walls, the palm trees, the cars, Mazda, Olds, the streets with holes, the stairways up to apartments, the second floor balcony, the kid running up the stairs, the rubber plant, hanging over the stairs, people everywhere struggling for a reasonable phone rate, lots of sex hap-pening...

A young man sits in a wheel chair, dressed like a gangster, baggy pants and bald head, dark T-shirt with the faces of comedy and tragedy air brushed on. He does not call it comedy and tragedy, he calls it, "Smile Now" and "Cry Later," which is kind of the same. He is going the other way, waiting for the bus, shot in the back, I assume. A pretty kid, square jaw and big eyes. He could be a leader, a lawyer, captain of the team. But not here. Here, he is paralyzed instead and waiting for the bus to pull down the cripple elevator, strap himself in, the whole bus watching, the driver uses the special key, every time a wheel chair gets on or off, it's a special little ceremony, a moment of strange silence, more silent than the bus usually is, those who were talking, stop, those who were staring out the window, look, and look away, secretly study the cripple, the soft lines in the face, the tin foil wrinkles around the eyes, hands, clothes, and you don't know what happened but you feel it. The chair gets locked in place, you look at your legs, grunt and then go back to your paper or staring out the window, and it is all very solemn.

I wonder if the kid still gets chicks? Can you have sex when you are paralyzed? Is he a hero on the street, his homeboys look to him like a saint, or a martyr, does he work it at the parties? You know, tell the story to the ladies, get all hard and crazy and then talk about the revenge. Or is life more cruel than that, he's got no legs so he's a freak, and no one wants to talk to him, say things like: "He's a freak now. His legs are all bent up, and skinny and shit. I don't like to be around him. He ain't the same."

Gangsters, Los Angeles folk stars, not giving a shit and

killing about it, killing themselves and their own and their families and anyone they are around, killing their culture, killing culture, making culture a killing thing, no poetry in these streets, nothing butterfly allowed, nothing open, it's all about the hard, the power, the muscle, and the tears they hide, "Smile Now, Cry Later," and that is America, it is the ghetto American swing, status-quo, nothing revolutionary, no change in the power structure, just hunt your brother, better than the Klan ever could. Why What Whatever.

America, Los Angeles, Mexico, can you all accept each other? America can you deal with your colors? Can you build your life for everyone that you are?

There is a Mexican woman wearing a medallion of the Virgen de Guadalupe, the Vision of Tepeyac. I love the Virgen, though I am not Mexican or Catholic. That does not matter, not to me. She is real. I have been to Her basilica in Mexico City. Outside the Church there are boa constrictors holding street preachers, Mexican Kabbalah occult prophets, Indio street kids selling boxes of chiclets. One girl, 8 years old, in Spanish asked me to buy her gum, I told her I already had some, "Well then why don't you give me a piece?!" she asked, put out her hand. Funny as hell, I laughed really good and gave her a bunch, and in the plaza there is vendor upon vendor selling Guadalupenated merchandise, yellow carnival booths selling Guadalupe on a rock, on a lighter, on a key chain, on a bottle opener, on a deck of cards, because she is divine, and is everywhere, and as you come into the Temple you can feel her presence at the door. There she is: the real deal, the one, the one Juan Diego saw. I entered and felt stupid, empty, the Vision was on the wall, I said something mean to my wife, I couldn't stand the beauty, I walked in with middle aged men, young Doc Martin wearing girls, grandmothers, rich and poor, walking on their knees to the altar, I took the wafer in her presence, religion did not matter, her body was all around us. I took a bite because she was blowing all over. The vision of truth and light. Her story says it all: she came to the slave peasant, living on the fresh stones of his fallen temples. You know the story, Juan Diego, an Indian, Aztec, walking in the granite of Mexico City, about ten years after the Conquest and the Night of Blood, he was walking in an area that had nothing, no water, no room for roots, dry and poor, and he was walking with his own roots, culture, world, destroyed, diseased and dead, gone living a nightmare, it must have been, infection, famine, destruction, pure despair without the love of sun, and to him, the poorest of the poor, comes the Vision of Truth beyond all of this world of battles and wars, to him comes the Goddess, the vapor of the earth itself coalescing into the form of a Vision and speaking to him, and growing roses for him to show the eyes of those who must know that there is a world beneath and above this domain of stone, a world that loves your blood and sings to you: Be. Be with all your might, my children. I am with you and will never leave you. I am with you in your blood, in your rivers of truth, your hands are the hands of Gods, not stones... build a life of the gods with them.

The Vision of the Virgen, not a sexual virgin, rather a pure pureness beyond physical forms, a vision of oneness, hermaphroditic truth serum from the sun, the fluid of all time and space and Juan Diego cried as we all cry in the presence of the Universe. Her eyes were too much for him or any man to bear. How could he be given this weight to know? Oh, please no, I cannot see this, it will surely kill me, I must be broken to understand. Oh, please kill me, I cannot stand. Oh, please kill me, I must be born. The truth will kill you because it is not from this world, it is toxic to this world, to live with it in you means certain death, anyone who says they know the truth, that they have it right here, that they are real and all of that, if they haven't died with the weight of their dream, then they lie.

I used to think, when I was really very high and thought I understood things like this, that the Virgen would appear on a wall, somewhere in Los Angeles, somewhere like MacArthur Park, at the Westlake Theatre swap-meet, or El Piojito discount store. I still think she will. For her children killing each other and themselves, wearing her tattooed on their arms, on their backs, feeling her tears radiating around their madman homicide/suicide sorrow, but then maybe this is the way it has to be, perhaps they are living and dying for something that I do not under-stand, or it is something that we all understand and it is too simple. Something like they need to bleed so that our world can have blood, lose blood and have blood, the dry white world of asphalt power needs blood, vampire style and this is the sacrifice. Or could it be that the dying cho-los do their world a service, heroes of the forgotten Mexican man and all who are forgotten. Everyone wants the togetherness that the cholo maimed brotherhood has, everyone, to be invulnerable to the attacks of others, to be willing and able to die for something that is truly yours, to have something that is truly your own, no matter how concrete or insignificant, and to kill for the same. Everyone knows what that is all about, in the world where money is the only power recognized, people long for power, more steel, more fiery, loud, something that will satisfy the flesh. Or maybe it is all about piling your bodies up on the doorstep of your enemy, saying "Here we are, do something." I think they die because they are forgotten, because they feel their lives are worth less than the jobs they can't get, the quarts of Malt they consume. Thus, the vision must come and bleed light onto the hearts of the fallen souls, who live to nourish the demons with their own blood. But when she comes will they listen, will they feel, know, or laugh in their jaded flesh cells, so hurt by everything, themselves, the law, the good times, each other, that the only thing that can touch them is a bullet? What a beautiful angel Death must be then, a wonder flower that we open into, taking us from the crippling wind of this sphere and clock. Come and take us, come and take our walls away. I want the true air breathed by lips without walls that kiss with beaded luna wings.

VINE STREET

YOSHINOYA BEEF BOWL, 24 HOURS, Mobil Gas, King of
Kings, Lord of Lords, Lenny Bruce, Hollywood and Vine
up the street, Clown Bazaar, Pic N Save, Lose Weight Get
Paid, 3rd Floor, telemarketing, pornography agents in the
upstairs room, Klieg lights looking for something, because
nothing is going on down here, change the channel, got a
dollar, wash ya windows, got a dollar, gonna have rain this
year, no man, that was last year, this year. Hey, man, what-
sa problem with you? Cars in the street, people at the corner, Flaming Hots from a bag, soda through a straw, the
air is a billboard, eggs, cheese, Bicycle Club Casino,
"Where It's At" it says. A man laying on the floor right in
front, "What's going on with you? Is anyone sitting
there?" On the bus going to score, pocket full of nickels,
pocket full of dimes, when I get to Cherokee gonna break
me off some... vomit, I wanna vomit, goddamn, can't
breathe, bad hamburger, stinkin' bus ride... the girl writing a letter, uses a different color for each word... "Are
you crazy?" "Yes, yes I am, does that bother you?" "It's
under that card, it's under that one." "No, you lose a five
dollars, baby." ...baby bouncing, jiggle jiggle, head on
mama's chichi... "I took one look at Chicago and got
right back on the plane. Insane, who could live there..."
lonely jazz street, Shelly Manne and his men, feeling Art
Pepper looking for murder in his own horn, Korean lady
singing nightclub, Mexican cowboy crying lonely in the

American streets, magician sparrows in the gloom. Expulsada de Mexico... llego, Tecate... The black Jerusalem man preaches the Apocalypse of Mind on the corner, nobody's listening... "The guy is so popular, people'd come if it was raining frogs, you know what I'm saying, right? You're not stupid, right? You know what I am saying, then? Good..." "No reason, I tell you, there is no reason—(pause)—I don't know, there's no reason..."

Vine street: movie stars, did that stuff ever happen? Who ever believed any of that shit? Who came here thinking those people were going to be on the corner? Let no one say that America has no religion. That is not so. What we have is religion that does not even pretend to matter, radio desperate nation, "Here at the corner of Hollywood and Vine..." A movie star walking by, "Say hello to the folks back in Kansas..." But there was no movie star on the corner, there was no corner. And Kansas came looking, trying to see the famous, the stars, the actors, the what? What are they looking for?

The movies suck, more now than ever, I say. The past has texture, it is enlightened even, it is evidence of something, of belief, of desire, of the lies that were believed, lies are nothing but truth, they are the need to believe something no matter what and that is the truth, that is what we are screaming at the moon in the darkness of our heads, everywhere, building empires of deceit, academies of pain, castles floating from our penis head, from forever, from Hindu lotus myths to Hollywood, lies so sweet, in their way, sweet lies, lies that show people longing for sweet emptiness, Jimmy Stewart, *It's A Wonderful Life*, what a sweet story about one man sacrificing for good things,

Miracle on 34th Street, how kind Mr. Kringle. Where are we now? What do we have that is better? Nothing. Hollywood has no soul, they could never produce something like a *Ben Hur,* or a *Ten Commandments.* I didn't really like the films, but they are so huge, big pictures, biblical, or *Spartacus* or even *The Godfather…* Now what? *Titanic?*

Hollywood had balls, big, greedy, monopolistic, fatal, ethnic oppressed Hebrew balls, now nothing. But of course, you see, I see, it is all about the place on the wheel of time. *The Ten Commandments* happened when it did because that's what was going on. Louie B. Mayer was looking down from Sinai Los Angeles, he was Moses, he had the promised land before him, golf club in one hand, car keys of the most powerful nation in the other.

And now we have *Titanic.* Think about that. Think about that fat sinking colossus of industrial hubris, everyone knew how the movie was going to end, what is the mystic vibe between the cracks of digitally mastered celluloid, why did we need to see this film, want to… I'll tell you why: our American asses are sinking, our world is sinking in cold, cold water, good looking kids, sexy chicks, poor people are going down, so you better believe it, the rich are gonna get the life boats, gonna survive, cyber mall mania, rich people in a bubble dome RV park while the rest of us suck on pesticide fumes and gutter punch.

The movies, take the light down off the wall, and look at what we are without it, faced with our big brains not being consumed by the light squiggling hypnotic puppet show, we would begin drawing cartoons on the bathroom curtains and chipping away, sculpting faces in the living room wall, and talking to them, perhaps we would even look at each other, and ask to know things about each other and about ourselves, or we would go insane, and kill each other for the lack of things we see there, we have always needed a force to mediate our existence into understanding, all of us have needed something, a third part or person or eye to direct the self, religion, art, love, we have always needed to think of ourselves in the ethereal next realm, in the place where the curses of reality cannot touch, we have always needed to go away from ourselves to know ourselves, and the strangest thing is that in these millennial years the world has created this extra dimension for people to access physically, through computers, films and drugs, but it is still not the place our souls rest, all of these things are manifestations of the need, but they are no more the place of soul than any car part or can of coke, it's just up there on the screen, telling you what to believe, entertaining the world into forgetting to believe anything, which maybe isn't such a bad thing.

What have our beliefs won for us, where have they taken us? To genocide? To destruction so massive no soul could contain you or forgive you? Better then to believe nothing, to just walk into the dark and not want anything but tits, or mud, or the facsimile of romance and passion, adventure, guns blasting holes in societies impotence, impotent because society is obsolete, obsolete because there is no more wilderness to conquer, there is no more real to become, now we are left with ourselves, and now we walk into the dark to see what we are, that is our culture, make with it what you can.

Hollywood is funny, we know more about these irrelevant movie star lives than we know about how our phone bill is figured, or how the city decides to post parking meters, or how legislation permitting jails to be built in your neighborhood is passed, or how toxic waste is created, or how the insane have come to live permanently on our city streets.

This town is full of actors, actors sweating out soul caca, acting like monkeys or door knobs or something. Acting is good, you feel something deep and then you meet the actor and they don't know what the hell they just did. But what do I care? I acted in high school. It made me insane. I felt too tall after I did it.

I did my first poetry reading on this street in 1984 at the Lhasa Club. A cool friend of mine asked me to read. What was I thinking? Why did I do it? Why do I do this? Somebody said they liked it. Yes, my literary career began right here. Because somebody said they liked it. One person. Mark that place with a "B," build a monument, mount a placard on the wall, tell the helicopter to shine its light this way. Build a message from the spot, dot the radar, here and then here, and now here as we move across the faces of the face that is the face of the Holy Shit Big Wow that is life stretching all across the sad blue sky.

HIGHLAND AVENUE

TWO GUYS SITTING OUTSIDE THE Donut Time. Probably came here from the Great White Way America, or maybe Lompoc or Riverside. Two young guys, long hair and a mohawk, leather jackets and dark, hollow circled eyes, tired and sad. This is fucked! They came out here to be movie stars and get the girl, get famous and forget... sounds cool, huh? Take my picture. Come on, I'm tragic. You know you want my tragedy in your camera. I'll tell you stories. Come on, don't I remind you of something? Don't you know me? Haha, come on. I freak you out, me and my buddy. We ain't cool. We ain't got no place, nothing going on. We came here 'cause... well, we don't know why, we just came. We thought, let's go and fuck around and meet some rich people who would do stuff for us, like you know, movies or some gig. Here comes the old man in his blue Olds. He comes for me after work, all the time. Freaky old man... one kid leaves and the other blows smoke and waits.

There it is, ADULT BOOKS, which means SEX. Sex is lovely, it is love, and like everything in this world it has been maligned by the energy of the dead-eyed fish sphincter that rules this sphere.

I've been to that porno shop. I've been to most of them in the city. I have been to these things in San Francisco and in New York, Times Square, baby. I remember back when the jack off booths in Los Angeles had doors. I guess that makes me old school. This here joint is a scummy joint. Which makes it just like the rest of the ones I've been in. There was a time when I went often to porn places, but then they took the doors off the booths and I got a VCR myself and just stopped going. Once in a while, before the VCR, I'd go anyway just to watch a porno movie. I'd be driving down the street, real late, like 4 or 5 in the morning, crackled wind, weary dereliction in the air, no one is out and no one should be, but there I would be driving around the city, looking for something, not friends, not people, waiting for the sun to rise. I'd read all the magazines, leered at the whores, and then I would end up checking out the porno pussy, taking my bent need to the back rooms.

This one joint up on Cahuenga and Hollywood, sight of an old jazz club and according to some book I read, the same address where Lenny Bruce did his thing way way back in the day, which made me feel better, walking in, looking around but not at anyone. The Mexican guy behind the counter checking me out, just seeing who I was. Then he'd go back to the conversation with his friends who had stopped by to hang out and look at pussy mags. I would buy some tokens, get a booth and check out a flick. By the booths, there'd be the hustlers, the kids of the street: stringy, long hair hesher blondes, no eyes for the light, head down, leaning on the back wall, as you went to watch your movie, late at night and nothing else to do, waiting for the sunrise, smoking all the air. Back then you could smoke places, smoke lots of places... smoke watching porno in Lenny Bruce's old joint with jazz ghosts and cum shots. And I'd just sit and watch some fucking or whatever and the queen hustlers would come by and check me out, see if I wanted them to suck my cock or if I wanted some ass. Really nice too. These guys would say, "Hi, can I help you?" Or, "Can I suck your cock?" "No, no, that's cool," I'd say. I never got mad. Why would I get mad? They were just trying to be nice. Then they'd leave and I'd do my thing and go, nodding satisfied with a cum high, feeling like a proper scumball freak in the Super Angel Cahuenga dog night. I always thought someone should make a movie of the place. Just let the cameras roll. Get close up on the faces. Look for the reasons.

Porno, it's all about jacking off to stupid, pure fucking. No love in sight. No soul, just empty cum and that is a great thing in its way. Jacking off, it is a great thing. Watching people fuck and jacking off to them fucking: it is despicably excellent. This is how I see it: these people are giving their pussies and cocks so that you may jack off. Sure they are getting paid and paid kinda well, but still you cannot price these things. They are sacrificing their nakedness. Giving it to you and your need. They aren't dry humping the world, mock acts of perversity meant to titillate the consumer into thinking they are extreme. This isn't MTV. This isn't Madonna. This is real unreality going to the wall, up the ass, taking it all, losing the hardest and looking the skankiest and it is what we are: fuckers. It's what makes the world so mad. I want it. I can't get it. I don't want you. I can't stand you. And it is all being done on TV.

The cock, the fat cock, which is really what men love to see, a good looking dick being sucked on, it's great.

Then it goes into the lovely honey pot. Everyone is screaming, everyone is sucking this and that... want to come just thinking about it. Fucking is nice. It is so nice that everyone wants it.

Everything happens when you are fucking—war is waged, childhood relived, oceans form, you become a mindless thing again, you are in the ocean, you are not wrong when you are fucking, fucking rules. I think we all agree, and movies about fucking, they make you come, make me come, want to come, and coming is nice too, coming is one of things what makes fucking so nice, getting warm and goofy, oh oh aah aha, yeah uhhhuhhh, head bobbing... Sex is more real than death, more feared. We really are animals and there would be mayhemic sex at every stoplight, in fact there would be no stoplight, hell if people fucked like they should there'd be no 7-11, no freeway, who'd have time for any of that stuff?

So there I would be, getting off, looking at the people, thinking they have given their sex up to the camera, they have given it up here, for me and my lonely rosy handed brethren, and as the camera gets close you see a speck of eye that shocks you, shocks you because it is clearly the speck of iris that is lost, that cannot be convinced that this is good, that what has just happened is for good, there is that fact in every porn fuck that it shouldn't happen, that it is a caged animal, a slave ship full, every one of those pussies belongs to someone who turned in their homework and wrote valentines to their mom, and now they are a body of idiot flesh being pumped full of hog for the butchers of lust. Pure exploitation, rape, meat rack, no love fucks. It is driven by another spirit, a mean and sad one. Sex is insane, it will always fuck us up and call us out. It is our belly need, the anger of our ages sweating through the mud of evolution, rage of gold, the rage of animal. We cannot let the animal loose, chain the fucker up. There is no chain can hold us. It is all out on the streets and walls. You cannot deny the dog.

We know the dog and the dog is us, balls to the wall. There should be nice places where you can go and take care of your business solo. I believe in masturbation. It is a good thing. It beats cheating on your love. There should be nice rooms. Pay a couple extra dollars for air conditioning. What if sex and masturbation and lust and desire weren't bad? What if fucking wasn't a sin? Would there be scummy porn joints full of sad seed desire? What if it was all normal? If porno was normal and famous people talked about it like they talk about movies or music, saying, "The reason I stayed in school was because of Sodomy class." Or, "Yeah, you know me and my friends used to make pornos in the garage. You know, kids' stuff. First we made them with our pets, you know, like most kids. We put little hats on the dog and well, you know, the rest is history." But it's not that way. All the porno people are bent, twisted, hardened in the heart, the women get used up, the men stay hard and lonely, they're all fucked up and fucked up is all there is to be. It is all this world has to offer. It is the only path of love this world has. Blunted, tweaked, fried, whacked, wasted, stoned. Drink the poison down, smoke the smut. But it doesn't work. None of it works, not for long. Not for real. You can't make the real when you are fucked up, all you can make is fucked up, you can't make a family and a wife, not me, get crazy when

I'm too much drinking, all these vices, the world's grip on you: they separate you from your love, yourself.

You can't come home and say, "Hi, Honey. just been hanging out at the Peep Show. Sure some fine vagina down there. Did a couple lines of speed after I jacked off, now I feel great. What's for dinner? How are the kids? Where are my socks? Have you seen my eyeballs? I need a new roto rooter. Do you got a cracked piece of glass I can saw my head off with? Ahhh, honey, what's wrong? It was just a line, just a joke. I didn't look that close." Nah, it's all shit.

What's good about sex is celestial, is hosanna lovely, it is Arcadian dew drops from outside the world of crime, how can a guy not get off watching people fuck, thinking about fucking? Men like to watch. We are watchers, watchers of baseball and history, the cosmos and the sea, so we sure as hell are gonna watch some fine ass bitches fucking a dude with a fine ass cock. Bitches and cocks, it's down to it. It's elevator to the bottom, no more floors. It's submarine flesh speak, gotta have some T-bone. Listen to me, I am flipping. Flipping pages of sex dream, bitch is a girl dog, cock is a rooster, a fucker, so it ain't about people, it's about dog fucking rooster rape, and we are this in a way that our minds will never understand and we are more than any fucking dog ass sodomite can ever get to with all his Larry Flynt jet streams of dream gone disease.

Oh, bad world of addictions, you fuck with me too much. You have fucked with my mind and left this stink in my veins. You know it is because I love nasty and need it that way. You know it is because I am insane. I want to slobber. My Johnson, my Albert, it has a will of sky-size

NOW. It wants to talk ionic, volcanic, irrational zones of must… stellar ejacula, vehicular luna, seaweed in the vein, the main vein. Oh, it is so good to be lovely with my lovely… I must meditate, get the body off of my mind, I must sit cross legged here and turn the bus into an ashram, a yoga center, I must get with new age music and bells, turn everyone on to saffron robes and gifts of orange. The loony lady sitting three seats away and the man with the hairy back will be holding sticks of incense and chanting something blissful in another language… I should begin a Gnostic sex cult that fucks its way to Sofia's first world of truth, white robed orgies of bearded new age perverts sucking and fucking the ordained white swan pussy.

Enough.

On the real: Porno is sad. I really wish it wasn't part of our world, but of course it is, this world is all about fucking and pain and death. The cocks, the ass, all the fun and sucking, it really turns me on and fucks me up. But what if my daughters did this? What if my little girls end up inside one of those shiny tit suits? What if that's them in there? What kind of illness bullshit is that? Fuck me and this sad world of lies.

The drunk kid who was touching the ladies hair like a freaky hunchback gets off the bus. He goes to the Donut Time and starts bumming change.

Hustlers and the lost abound, people, destroyed in this, the First World.

This nation has destroyed more than it can ever admit. America, you are in pain as bright as your lights, as loud as your music, as big as your highways, as high as your buildings, as far as your rockets can go, you are blind to the sorrow you are running from. America, I am sad for you, full of Empire and nothing, freedom to run from your demons. If you never heal this wound you will never be whole and what of us, all of us, who are called Americans? Haha, what then?

America, all your heroes and saints are full of shit.

We are always gonna hate each other. Everything is always gonna be the other guy's fault. The white man this, the wetback did it, the Chinaman smells, the nigger is gonna kill me... No one is ever gonna get past it. How can we? It is who we are. We are always gonna want to eat shit and screw the other guy so that we can do it and blame him when it makes us sick. God bless America, the land of multi-colored rage where the only thing to burn, when no one cares, when nothing burns, is yourself.

What would go down if there was no more USA law and order holding the system into place? I mean what if it wasn't there? Gone, deteriorated, no teeth, nothing. What would happen, then? Would it be Kosovo and all that mad shit, waves of insanity, ending in Ethnic Cleansing... I don't think so? Or I do. I hear the ringing and I don't know what it is. No, I think people are down for making it work, ultimately, I think people are into making a new people. Because? There is no choice. Oh, that's cool, I say to myself and relax and scratch my head.

The streets flip past, the bus stops at a red light, I imagine cutting everyone's hair in their sleep. I think about the last time I ate. I think what if the bus was a cult thing and to get off was to kill yourself, so every time someone got off they dropped dead, old ladies and school kids, "I am getting off here." and they step off and suck poison. "Ahhh, I go to a better place." Or what if the bus was life, like I think it is anyway, and where you get off is where you are born, you step off the bus a smelly middle aged alcoholic and onto the street you fall, a wailing infant, purple toes with an umbilical cord wrapped around your neck. "Where's your momma, little fellow?" ask the people on the street. But they are your parents, they will raise you and love you and abuse you with their love. The streets, the places, the doorways, the windows, the tires, the finger nails, the contaminated sky, all will raise you as their own. You look back from the bus and the sidewalks are littered with corpses and infants. A whole tribe is born this way. They have no identity. They were given no papers anyplace, no bus pass. They know they were born on a bus and that is all. They roam the streets, from bus line to bus line looking for the bus they are from.

The lady with Guadalupe around her neck gets off the bus.

Odessa Market. Poinsettia Liquor. They used to have a tire shop with a big statue of a mechanic in a bow tie holding a couple of tires. He's not there right now. Now it's a Russian grocery. That's cool. Downtown they had the Chicken Boy on Broadway—a big chicken headed fiberglass adolescent standing straddle legged over that great street. The tire man, he is gone. The downtown chicken boy, gone too. Argos Fiberglass Rooster, crowing for the coffee shop nation to wake up and eat some bad buttermilk hot cakes—gone. All gone, greasy love secrets. When did this city become so together? When did I? We are all changing together.

Oh, I feel the ghosts of Oki Dog, Okinawa Hot Dog. Oklahoma Lost Dog. It's Okay Dog, it's an oki dog day. Every oki dog will have its day. The Oki Dog, the metaphor struck me right away, a big spoon of chili, a few slices of pastrami, two hot dogs, maybe something else, I don't recall, all wrapped up in a flour tortilla, burrito style.

The Mythic Land of the Oki Dog. The owner was some big Okinawan guy who lorded over the place like a kind of cult leader, he wore big sun glasses, let the runaway kids hang out all night, some kind of glory, a burgerdom of oil drum potted rubber plants and spacey vines, the expression of Yes, let it all happen, the inner mind of some kind of sleepy eye of love. I mean, it was just let happen, all manner of Runyon Canyon devil worshipper, down and out 1970s singer/songwriter, disco flotsam, sex hunter, American wasted youth, all sipping soda, eating fries, living many dog years in their eyes. They all would come down from the hills, out from the shitty apartments, from the alleys, from the recording studios, from their parents' house, from the bus station, from the hotel, from the dumpster, from the backseat, from the club, from the bathroom, from the moon, from the sun, from the space ship in the desert, from the devil's hole, from the dog pound, from the squad car, from prison, from the hospital, from the morgue, from Dixie land, lala land, the Golden Rest Home, from the black eye bar, from the number four bus, and it was open all day and night.

All this alternative culture consumerism, it is just another Jell-O mold. It all sells out. It all becomes something else.

It all becomes safe. It all turns into a TV show, a commodity, a price tag, a group deal, a pair of pants, shoes and a jacket, hair and a car. Poor Americans, all we know how to do is turn things into commodities. It ain't real if you can't sell it. It isn't important if it isn't a billboard splattered all over the coffin shaped like culture. Everyone is safe, even the suicidal motherfuckers, they are not taking any chances, they're just doing what society has scripted for them. There's no risk in fucking up, it's just suicide. Risk, risk is living and trying to make that work. It is pure risk. Insanity. Trying to make something meaningful in this meaningless world. Live a free life, one that hasn't been packaged already, doing something 'cause you love it, not looking for the world's approval, anyone's approval, or anyone's lead, just doing the bidding of your veins and the harbors therein, breathe your ghost into the machine. That'll really cripple the pigs, jack the fashion lords, derail the fascists. Yeah.

Stanley Street where I did my laundry. I believe I had sex in a car somewhere around here. Yes, with a girl named Beverly. It was hot. She screamed things, nice things, hot things. She made me feel like a fella. I went out with her a few times too. Stayed at her house when her folks were gone. We watched *The Chosen*, a good movie about Jews in New York around the time of the war, she tripped on me when I told her my great grandmother came to the west in a covered wagon. Never met anyone whose family actually did that. Neither have I. American me. Got mad when I wouldn't buy her a hot dog. Sex meant I was supposed to buy her stuff to eat. "When I go out, I get fed." I didn't know what she wanted to eat. I swear. Punched me in the arm. That was the end of that.

Cathy, my wife, is funny. We'll be driving around town and she'll just blurt out, "I had sex on that street. I did it there. I did it in that parking lot." It turns me on. I don't know why. I get off on the idea of her, not the idea, the fact of her getting it on with someone else and I walk in and get in on the action, come, scream and yell and then kill everyone in the room. I would kill the guy. Bash his brains out and fuck him in the eye. And her, her I will give her a stern talking too and ask her if I can film it next time. Please, baby, what the hell did we get the video camera for?

The Tom Kat movie theatre, Spike, long time leather bar, two guys run out of the bar beating each other on the head. Everyone looks. They want to kill each other. Some other men come out of the bar and stop the fight. Both men are crying. One is bleeding where he was hit by a cue ball.

FAIRFAX AVENUE

FAIRFAX IS FOOD, AND THAT makes it a holy street, that and the fact that it is one of the hearts of Hebrew Los Angeles. A few old people get off the bus. I wonder if any of them lived in Boyle Heights when they were kids. This is the beginning of the Holy Day, the day to begin again, to count the past and hold the ones you love. Are these old people going to temple, or are they too long on this earth to believe in anything besides themselves? The sun, not all the way down, is calling like a canter and the palm trees are davening, the streets are kneeling to the ground, the walls are bent eyes closed tight, looking deeply into their hands. Fairfax Chabad, the Hassidim pray at dawn, old men in big beards, kissing the Scripture, weeping over the Torah as it brings them life in its words, words that live and make live, in the beginning was the word and thus life is spoken here.

Fairfax: Canter's Delicatessen, nightclub cigarettes, seeing what each other look like in the light, clankin' and clinkin' coffee cups, singing, show stopper, listen to me sing, Summertime, at 4am, want to know what your thinking, baby, in the second act it all fell apart, okay but I really liked the way the play became physical, I really like the way memory is an act itself. I dig the fact that we are never not in any part of our lives. I dig how it comes unglued from something in the sky, this invisible muscle of memory, it always sits there like a smell, something waiting to

114

be touched, to come in, and it comes as it will, strange trees on the ceiling, trying to figure what they were. Many have sat high on psychedelics staring at that ceiling pattern, and made good with a friend in the bathroom, getting high, getting down, going to the toilet, feeling like a prince, because Canter's is princely. It smells princely.

Farmer's Market is down the street, too. Oh, lovely employer that it was. I worked there cutting sandwiches and making Jambalaya. I was a good cook. I was a madman. I would yell and scream and dance around the kitchen. The gay waiters wanted my body. The ladies longed for it too. Men customers would jump out of their seats and point at me and give me the scary eye. Girls left their phone numbers. I coulda been some kind of sex god. I coulda had a line out the door, speaking broken Spanish, good for a white guy though, don't give me any shit, I got bilingue in heaven. Partied at Filiberto's house. Mid-Wilshire, dancing in his sister's living room down in K-Town Oaxaca tenement, week night birthday bash, kids up late with the drunk adults. There was no homework in the poverty of joy.

It was cool. I was alright in the finger-cutting, arm-burning hard work, cooked for a handful of years, all told, in Santa Monica and Santa Cruz and here in Los Angeles, a year at Farmer's Market and then two more at Mrs. Gooch's Market. Farmer's Market. What about Farmer's Market? Old School Hollywood Americana. It is a love spot on the cancerous face of the city. The trinkets are terrible and the fruit, it all shines. Survivors sip coffee. The post cards are lewd and the old Hollywood cowboy strolls with his collection of buttons pinned all over his hat, sips his tea, his lemonade, leaves his story in the wings and nest of the pigeons, leaves his story in the silent paw prints of the after hours kitty cats that live on the roof.

Fairfax: the fat lady of Fairfax had her cat in the box and her shopping cart full of feathers and paper and a suitcase of blue. Roz from New Orleans wanted to rescue the cat from being trapped by the fat lady. "No," I said. "It's her friend." It was. It wasn't cool. Roz was right. It was no good for the cat who had only one eye, but I could just see the lady talking to her cat in the box. We don't know the story. It was a messed up cat, but who knows? I mean, the lady was caring for it in pizza bum lady fashion... Whatever, I haven't got pizza from there in a while.

In my mind I see Canter's big green neon lettered sign, above us on the street, me and my friends, we were young talkers, young seers, so full of the really, the really of poetry, the really of love, soul things, blood style hunger for the moon streets of naked you, the really where the inside begins 911 Angel choirs rattling libraries in a paper cup moving down a street of the night inside, an empty hand pushing the crosswalk button of life, really high, love potion, yes I mean really, like, talking to some girls trying to make time, make jokes, make friends, make the bed, make up your mind, make someone else pay for the food you just ate, fall in love, fall in love.

Back then it was all about being downtown and seeing the city so full of sad love, love so sweet it cracked the green dawn razor blades around streets, a tree of sparrows spilling into the San Julian eye of some beat punk rock painter, some one who wants to paint the name of God, crazy, like that, messed up, brick walls, seeing his name in the train track gloom, angels kiss the hair, anointed greasy, kiss his eye, and his eye dancing with the queens of the LA River, ghostly things, which everyone feels, at any river, anywhere, but here this river is the ghost of a river, this river calls gurgle, churn churn laugh laugh deep alluvial courses from beneath the concrete of WE FORGOT. There's ghost in that there water!! Painting the Chapel of Man in the City of Suns, and in the moment of benediction, he was a body become dusted flesh laid out across all the stratum of moment: blessed is he who disappears in the weeded dream of night, brushing derelict train track Chinatown and rail road streets with the paint of veins (his people, his angels, his demons), blessed is he who knows the secret canvas that moves all around the world.

One night, just out of high school, on top of the Wilshire Royal with Dave Martin and Dave Reiker, people I haven't seen in a while, in another life really, not really, and some girl that dated Robert DeNiro and I don't believe her, and we are drinking on the roof, and I look out over the park and the downtown skyline, and it is city I am looking at, a maze of pipes and poison and I look down and see Al's 24 hour coffee shop and 24 strikes me as the kindest number, the most vulnerable, always there, open like the love of Jesus' Father, 24, double twelve, a year of daylight and a year of night, one embracing the other, one holding up the other, one slipping into and seducing the other, but always on opposite sides of the glass, and I see the 6th and Rampart Car Wash, the one featured in the movie, it is long gone now, but then, 1986, it was still there, and I was proud, proud of my city in the middle of the night, looking down on the eternity of coffee shops and car washes. I was Whitman looking at his Manhattan. I was Neruda gazing at Macchu Picchu, Miller in Paris, Marvin Gaye in the midst of ass, Emily D. staring at her dead cat, Simon Rodia staring at a blue broken bottle of Milk of Magnesia and seeing towers of light. I was there, the place of all places... I was in.

Fairfax, street of old ladies, we are going now. Where are we going? Just to get a car, the rest cannot be told. The back seats are empty, written on, the windows you can't see through, written on too, what for, a part of the seen constellation, a billboard of your own, "Here I am. Here I am. Hanging from the freeway sign."

Why not? The Hollywood sign stuck official graffiti in the middle of the hill, where everyone can see it. It's all about the light out here, billboards glowing against a orange clouded night. Why not? Play the music loud. We've been here forever. Clean and chrome the car. In this city, everyone is a star. Thus spake the Summer.

Who really knows what this earth is all about?

There is another drunk guy walking down the street. Oh, is he drunk! Goddamn, ooh, hit the wall, oh oh, there he's going again, walking again, his head in the fish tank. Sit down, man, sit down, the sheriff's gonna get ya. Get off the street. Women are walking down the street. There are some people in nice cars. It must be nice to have a nice car. I know it is. I want all the things the world offers. I want, I want things, I want to possess riches, I am like everyone in that way, I see the fine clothes and fine fabrics, and the fine wines and the fine wall papers and the fine shoes, and the fine tooth brushes, the fine stockings, the suits of armor, the dining room sets. I see these things. I want the car, I want to be a contestant, I want to ride through the night, zooming on the freeway in a fine car, fine things are fancy at the mall, so sit down and watch all the people. Reality is at the mall, that is where all the people are hanging out these days, that is where humanity goes. Running, bustling, talking, gesticulating with food in the mouths and a run in their stockings, listening to someone but not listening to them, listening to the hum of the crowd because they think they hear someone or something in it calling their name.

"Sharon, Sharon," they hear and their friend goes, "Are you listening to me?"

"What, huh, yeah, of course, it's too bad."

"What's too bad? I wasn't saying anything was too bad."

"Oh I don't know. What were you saying?"

"Nothing."

The friend is mad, hurt really, she can't even hear herself in this loud stupid world and her so called friend totally ignores her.

"I have to go," she says and leaves with her bag, leaving her coffee on the table.

"Wait, let's talk, later, again, it's nice seeing you."

"Call me," the mad friend says over her shoulder and continues into the crowd, the humming buzzing crowd, the inattentive friend watches her, and forgets what she looks like, forgets what she is looking at, turns her head and tries to get closer to the noise that is her name. But she can't because it's like a noise you hear, underwater in a pool. It is in your ear, it is all around you but it isn't com-

ing from anywhere. So she leaves and forgets her bag.
What if I was gay? Man, I wouldn't make it. Maybe a couple of flings, but they'd kick me out or want to turn me out with the trade on the East end. I would get all heart broken, get pissed off and fuck somebody up and get my head split in the process, I can see it all now, like those guys at the bar.

"What are you doing with him?"

"Fuck you, you're sick, you fart all the time, you snore, you can't even suck cock."

"Fuck you, I'll kill you, you bitch, you fucking bitch…"

I break into heart broken violence, bust a cap and split and go cruise the streets looking for John Honey, get murderous bath house fucking liquor store garbage can drunk fast and troubled. You see, it wouldn't work for me. So forget it.

The drunk guy walking down the street is an actor. I can tell. He's wearing penny loafers with no socks, a button shirt and some dirty nice pants, some quality garments but they are dirty and he's dirty. He looks like Malcolm Lowry. Or what I think Malcolm Lowry should look like since I have never seen even a picture of the guy. I figure he is basically nice looking and he is fucked up, and so is this guy. His face is red and he is walking on his toes. He is lit. He looks great. It looks like a movie. You know, Boston boy misfit rich kid, always trying to sing to things that aren't there, family doesn't understand, moves to California to get loose and get lost. What's he tell the folks he's doing? He tells them he's an actor, he's sent them his 8x10, he's good enough looking. He can talk fine, so he's an actor, gets an agent does a commercial for... for... AT&T... for Taco Bell, does a play, he plays a bum, he found himself then, but hasn't worked in a while. It's the drinking. He's unreliable, but he's been writing poetry and getting drunk, smoking menthols, smoking Kools, writing weird poems, on little bits of paper, taking the bus late at night down to the beach and watching the waves, he wants to cry, he wants to laugh, he does both, he passes out, he gets arrested in Santa Monica for drunk and disorderly then gets out, gets a drink, drinks it in the alley with his penny loafers on and his Brooks Brother shirt. Now he's walking back to his apartment, but he lost the key so he's going down to the bar where he asked the bartender to hold his spare. Good thinking. I would never have thought of that. So I pass by on the bus and see him and say, "Looka that guy, whatta lush."

This is a city of losers. I think about this in West Hollywood because I see so many actors on the street. The Headshot People, those who come here and hate it and themselves and drink overpriced drinks and complain about how phony everyone is and they point out the fact that this city has always attracted and supported those who couldn't make it elsewhere. Take for example, Otis Gray, the guy who built Los Angeles, who made the LA Times, he was a Midwest Lame, lost it all selling vitamins and then stumbled into Los Angeles and became the builder of the Empire. Film, the movies, they all ran out here to set up shop far away and not get popped by the Feds. They came out here and built up the world they wanted to live in. They stretched the canvas and built themselves. Los Angeles, Hick Jerusalem, Babylon

Hollywood, the outlaw empire of artifice the vision of America from Russian immigrant Jews who were never let in. America the hallucinated.

LA wasn't even a city until the movies came, it was burnt, hicks at the beach, nothing more, couldn't find a sandwich after 8pm. We built this city...

The Chinese Theatre. I put my feet in the foot prints, and I was struck by how real it was there, I mean it, real, authentic, folk, the theatre is aged, the upper walls are faded, paint is peeling, the years have made it meaningful, even as a shrine to facade and empty glamour, but what is so empty about it? The people come and they see the names of the Marx Brothers. Who is more real than they? And Gene Kelley, didn't he dance in the rain? The Chinese letters, red lights all over the place, a touchstone. A collective symbol, being, our culture, the shadowed language that comes from the screen is a ground that is beyond us and between us, a history, like I was saying, not of battle or achievement, freedom or knowledge, not the story of a people, it is a history of an extra world that has been driving this century of speed, seeing in the dark, the interior consciousness of the masses. Frank Sinatra's foot prints are really there and they belong to America like the Cherry tree, and John Henry's train.

Old ago Hollywood, still fruit, still a ranch. Can't you see it? And with these crazed filmmakers roaming the palm tree lanes of promise like marbles across a monopoly game board that had been left in the sun. These nuts bent the neon that beckoned the cowboy to smoke his Camel in the Lost Angel Hot Dog night, but you know the city, the Angel, it spun them in its direction, Far West, they came with an idea in their head and then the sunlight, the long sky and the end of the road, the big water, it messed with them. They got scared of themselves at the end of the continent, and they had nothing to face but naked, alien, desire, and they were lost, all built from madness in this land of jeering wildflowers.

LA CIENIGA BOULEVARD

THE BUS GOES BY WHAT used to be what used to be, buildings on the corner, emblems of social moods. In the Disco late Seventies, Flipper's Roller Boogie Palace. In the New Wave Eighties, an Esprit store. Now, it is a Sav-on Drugstore. Sav-on Drugstore. Sav-on Drugstore, Sav-on!

I love a good Sav-on. It amazes me how high to the sky the aisles of pain relievers reach, and the cosmetic counter and the cheap alcohol. Alcohol, my family's demise. You know it is funny how good it feels at first. How much love you feel when you first start getting high, how much God you feel, how all over the world you feel, how frickin' French and noble you get to be, but then, after awhile, it is all about waking up hung over and pissed off at your kids, getting bugged by the way your wife pours coffee and you freak out and break the remote control and then fall on your ass and look at the pieces of broken remote control and your kid staring at you like she doesn't know what the hell you are and you try to tape the remote back together, pick up the pieces, find the tape, but it doesn't work—you can't change the channels, you lose, you broke it, you gotta buy a new one, you gotta live with the mess.

Ice Cream at Sav-on. That is where it's really at, made this country great.

Motorcycles of love I do recall, that moved between cars, across a GoGo's Los Angeles, nighttime, the city was weak in the stomach and two muscled tank top boys, sun

124

tan, good hair, leaning into the night and chasing each other on their bikes, between all the traffic, terrific, ass wanting rabbit for the stew, sex air, all the air we ever breathe, cigarettes brought on platters of the wind, and it is symbolic, the motorcycles glide between blind shields of the straight man worlds and they don't care, and they do it for everyone, beautiful and fast, the whole world is with them in their fuck and in their motorcycle chase and in their leaving blues, and these chasing boys are beautiful, not because they are nice to look at, but because they want, and that is why the sky cries, that is why I see tear drop stains everywhere, shut up and listen, this world is a tear, we live inside a tear, every breath that we take is the shape of a tear, rain and snow, the grains of sand, the molten bends of the substrata, the bead of come, the shape of the fetus, and amniotic sack, the eyes of the dead, the cup in the palm of your hand, all are tear drops, tear drops, for grief and life taken, and as I see it, life given. We drive on.

My image of the Tropicana Hotel: teenage quaaluded Mckenzie Phillips freaks out at the pool side with Rodney Bingenheimer telling her just get it out, get it out, and Tom Waits leaning on the balcony watching, Ricky Lee calling him from the room, "What are you doing?"

"I'll be right there, I'm just... uh... checking on the kids."

How come AIDS never got big with bigots in Georgia or took out a senator or a bank president?

What if the world understood itself? What would it be like if it was alright being gay, wanting sex, being sad or feeling so alive you couldn't get out of bed for three days? What if the one who heard voices was made special counsel to the mayor, or was the mayor? What if the bars were open all night? What if there was a government job called Minister of Sexual Affairs? What would the world look like if the world could deal with people? What would people look like if they could deal with themselves, you know, just accept everything?

Santa Monica Blvd. Halloween. Got my crotch grabbed by a drag Madonna when I came here in 1990. "Are you straight?" "Yes," I said, and felt bad, felt like I was cheating. What was I doing here, turning on Madonna? And I wasn't even gonna give any. I am sorry, Madonna Man. I love you anyway.

AIDS, a many winged conspiracy to destroy the humans who fucked too much, really shook the pillars. Tells you where the real seat of power lies. I bet you Sodom and Gomorra was this: a happening couple of gay cities and the powers that be trapped all the gay people in there and set the places on fire. Sexual Genocide. And then AIDS happened and put death in our love, not just disease, but a bad kinda dying.

Check this out: a huge transvestite with big tits wobbling drunk in huge heels and big wig is taking a picture of herself, head tilted back, mouth open, tongue apparent, leaning in the doorway of a closed store.

In Wyoming they crucified that boy. Bet they had him suck them off first before they ripped him up.

The gay man threatens the all powerful god and country. How can sucking cock do this? I do not know.

Jesus gets on the bus. He looks at me. He nods. "My

friend, you are looking dashing tonight," he says. "Where are you going?"

"I am going to pick up my car, haven't you been following along, don't you see all?"

"Yes, yes, I do see all."

"Why do you show up now? I didn't call for you. I did before but that was when I thought I was gonna die. Am I gonna die? Is that why you came on the bus? Is that why you are here? Now? Why now?"

"I want to HAVE SEX with you."

"What?" I knew it, gay, watching me masturbate all these years.

"Oh, forget it. Nothing." He retracts quickly. Jesus is pissed off.

"What? What's going on." I blew it. The Son of God wanted me and I missed it. All I did was argue.

I love Jesus. Always have loved Jesus. His love came from the blood, cured the sick and made the broken whole, brought peace to the ravaged, taught the soul to live when the body could not, Love his God, a river that bleeds through us and beyond our graveyard prayers.

"Jesus, are you really the Son of God and what exactly does that mean?"

"I don't know."

"Whatta ya mean you don't know?"

"I mean I said that a long time ago, I don't even remember what was going on."

"Well, have you seen yourself on TV?"

"Yes."

"Whatta you think?"

"Oh hell, what can I do about it. People do what they

want finally. I become whatever they need."

Jesus walks on the street and he is sad, because he has been turned into a Pro Wrestler with big muscles. It is hard to walk like this. But it is what they want.

"Jesus, you are heavy in the store fronts of Latin Los Angeles. You aren't so bulky there. You're different there, I don't know how to explain it. Hands waving, heads bowed. The poor people need your broken heart."

He doesn't say anything.

Rodeo Drive

HERE WE ARE IN THE driveways of plenty where everyone wants to BE...

Who are the people with lawn jockeys?

It is here that I think of Downtown, Skid Row, the Nickel and San Julian, Towne, Los Angeles, Midnight Mission, Toy District, Boxland, rows upon life, after face after face of men and women in cardboard... it is insane, truly unreal, wound speaking sacrificial bone piles to the moon, a fire that burns on human blood, it is symbolic, it is representational, it means exactly what you think it means. The world consumes. If it cannot consume your money, it will consume you.

The rich are there 'cause the poor are there.

There is nowhere to go in the land of opportunity, there is no up, there is only more. The poor dream that the rich have it all, but the rich have nothing, and everyone knows this. The poor, miles and worlds away from these mansions, they know it. Can you imagine being last in a losing game? Go insane or quit. The soul knows all this. Whether anyone admits it or not. It is all there.

I did make a Sandwich for Lauren Bacall, yes, I did do that when I worked at Ms. Gooch's Market, here in Beverly Hills, that was cool.

Look at these palm tree lined streets. This is what it is all about: Sunny California, boring, fat free. Timothy Leary lived for many years up in the hills around here. I went to Leary's seventy-fifth and final birthday party. Got my picture taken. I was invited with some friends to read poetry. The chick who told us to come and read said it was going to be an intimate affair with about 50 people, like, you know, Jack Nicholson and Quentin Tarantino. Cool, I thought, check out the Hollywood head cheese scene, shit, who knows, maybe I'll make a million dollars 'cause I'm so fuckin' cool. My brilliance will be lauded, I will be asked to give private instruction and read the verse of Shelley and Yeats to Nicholson's children. I will win a part in a Tarantino movie being a poetic assassin. "This is the money of my reason. I shall have my money, man, and thou shalt pay my dreams well." Blam Blam Blam. I should be rich. I should be insane with my dollars. I wanna have cash so I don't have to work. Just walk around the park all day, sip absinthe, play Barbies with Penelope, eat cherries, write poems, make long hours of love with my lady, smoke, drink, and just not work. To be giddy with uselessness. Not have to do anything, don't have to try, your kids never feel the stress of the real world, they go to freaked out private schools, and take the best drugs and have the best, most articulate, problems and the finest therapy and you are out of it, you can't relate to anyone, you are not a normal person, you long for normalcy, you denigrate yourself to achieve this, you think being twisted, sexually perverse will help you understand yourself and the world better, you are wrong but you destroy your life trying. Whatever, I really want those easy breathing dollars.

It didn't work out. The party was huge. 500 people, at least. Tony Curtis was there being interviewed by a TV

camera, all lit up amidst the lawn of people and his plat-
inum blonde bomb-shell girlfriend, half his age, one third
his age. He was doing it. Completely. I don't even know if
she was real. Silver haired, Rat Pack, Boheme Brooklyn
swinger, now a painter, lover of fine pleasures, good
things. I think he played it as good as any of them. I mean,
I watch interviews with him and he seems to know what's
up. He seems to have his mind intact and you know, getting older and turning into a painter, wearing sandals, all
good choices. Tony Curtis at Tim Leary's last birthday—
True Hollywood Stories. It was sick. So sick it was awesome.

Forget poetry, I thought, I want to pimp out, party, get
stupid, forget that poetry shit, no one is listening, I don't
have anything to say to these people. They don't wanna
hear words, they don't want to hear about the mist of
freak love when there is a tank of nitrous oxide and Perry
Farrell walking around. I ended up at the nitrous tank
myself, sucking down balloons and watching the foggy
hills cave in and then explode as if the world was taking a
breath and everything was being sucked into its mouth
like a spaced out whirlpool with all the Lucky Charm con-
stellations spinning around and around the central black
hole of the sky and then, boom! The air comes back into
my head and I am sitting on the grass with Anthony
Ausgang, "I'm having a kid." My life was jumping from
BC to AD. I looked up and there were all these guys
around the nitrous tank, pressing and reaching and grabbing and pushing and generally freaking out like hungry
fish. What does it all mean?

Eventually we got to read our poetry, me and my

friends. It was stupid but it was cool, our little gift to Mr. Leary. Not that he needed it or wanted it. I read really quietly, soaking in the absurdity of it all. It was ridiculous. I was the nut on the corner, the evangelical insane person who screams and yells, but more ridiculous, because it was at a party. I'm having a kid. I'm gonna be a father. What am I doing here? Tim Leary was a freaky old man who had his mind in the super electro blip. I mean, he was loaded on what, I don't know. He looked happy, high on cancer, walking around with his balloons of nitrous. It had all worked out. He wasn't homeless. People still said, "Hi." Life was behind him, he was zonked with a death laden mind. He was going out of this life spun free.

I thought the party would be saturated with LSD. It wasn't deep like that. No freaky people staring at glowing paintings or watching whacked out skateboard movies with sex change operation footage spliced in just to warp you into panic. None of that. No Jell-O slide or orgiastic grope sessions. Not for me. A mere mortal. Perhaps behind some secret handshake doorway Terrence McKenna was slapping Madonna in the tantra of golden rose showers. But for me, nope, I didn't see any of that.

All that psychedelic sixties, what kind of freedom did it grow? What lasts from it? An accelerated drug culture, a shallow, need-a-fix culture. Perhaps this is the best that we could do. You know, saying, "Well, this fucked up America is never going to be a deep place, not real and deep, it is deep but deep in plastic and fantasy, so here are some cookies that will blow your four lane mind right out of the front seat, but we will all keep on driving the beast into the apocalypse."

Something started, happened in the Sixties, no doubt, the bottle got broken, stuff started to pour out, America was going insane. It saw itself. It opened. It was open, for sure, you can tell, but then what? The pendulum swings, as dear Danny Wize used to say. People died, people got tired, things changed, things grew up. For sure the world is different now than it was before. Not because of hippies but because of all the things that were exploding. America had to die. The Empire had to fall. Okay, not fall as in gone, but there's no blind America "White is Right" line of blood thought in the mass mind of these states. Sure, it exists, but we know it exists, we are aware, even the racists must take the 18th of January off and watch news clips of "I Have a Dream." All the voices of America can be heard on the radio. At least on my radio. Oh please, not all, let some be safe. But if you ain't heard then you ain't heard. 1993, UCLA, Chicano Studies Protest, Faculty Center Sit-In, the cops come to take us away. The TV cameras were there. The cops tell them to leave. We scream and yell, "No, hell no." Because we know what it means to be not seen by the recognizing eye. Okay? So Now, end of century, millennia number two, we all know each other are human beings and shall be loved and hated, murdered and birthed as human beings.

I will say this, though, psychedelics were good for me. They broke my head open and dangled me from a string that wasn't there. It is good. Do them. See the absurdity of all this tight and true reality. Laugh at the face on the dollar and the shape of the numbers. Let the roof become a big cow tit and the lights, bright nipples, and you are just a babe in the suckling womb as you lay on the floor of a naked and kind beast you have never seen before or ever will again. And you are the only one in your vision, everyone else seeing their own demons and angels. Yes, open it all and live orbiting around the sun itself. All becomes a much bigger thing when your brain's channels of reason and right stop working. Synapses letting truckloads of indecipherable images into your head: candy bar, burger, headlight, mother's face, liquor store, market aisles, stacks of Campbell's Soup cans, none of it fitting, making any sense, clouds puffing smoke and charging across the sky as teddy bears and rhinoceroses and you better be around cool people or you might feel real bad when the world of your world crumbles, terror, horror train you can't get off in your blood, just make it stop, make it stop. The Evil Queen is in the shower and on the curtain, a million tiny smiling evil queen faces on each fiber of the carpet, whose carpet, where carpet, what is carpet, why is it here? Who needs this? Who put that dog there? Is it really there? Oh, I don't have a dog. If I just laugh, it will go away… and you laugh and it just walks away and you go outside and see the sidewalk full of veins, everywhere you look everything is stitched with the strata of karmic dimensions, looking very Hindu, all of it, full, even the dark sparkles and twists, mushroom clouds and the tongue of fear.

I did learn this: In the house of my fear, I was the only one there, keeping it open.

Tim Leary died that next year. I hope he is where he wanted to be. I had fun at your party. One week later my first daughter was born on planet Earth, for real.

The bus is close to empty, a handful of people, an office

lady reading a book, a couple lady bums, the bus is in another world now: Century City, Avenue of the Stars. The bus is an invader from the other side of town, the single conduit between the worlds of the server and the served. Scratched up seats and rattling windows. It moves like an alien dog through the clean shrubs, picking up the people who work holding up The Cheese and making Jacuzzis, taking care of children that are not their own. If it wasn't for this here bus Steven Spielberg would not have a jacuzzi, thus such great films as *Shindler's List* would not get made. Think about that. The driver has stopped calling out streets and is driving faster. No one is going to work right now.

The tension of the city is gone. The sidewalk is fat and empty. The streets are full of commuters. The tension of poverty gives way to the paranoia of affluence. Money, you have to have it, can't have enough, do anything to get it, crawl like a rat across a hostile border to pluck chickens for 4 bucks an hour. American money must be good money.

America, the Unbelievable. America, the Useful Fantastic Excalibur Birth Control Virtual Dog of the Future. America, the rock and roll disco sissy killer. America, a handful of Advil and a gun full of plastic sauce. America, just a fun place to lose your mind and find your ass in debt. Here we are, dropping the bombs of economical justice on the humans who won't let business run its course. Serbia, stop the genocide so we can safely put McDonald's there. America, blessed by an unholy god, giving the gift of demons to kill and not know blood.

Santa Monica Blvd. train tracks. A train used to run

right down the middle of the street. I walked there. New Year's Day, 1985, a senior in high school, going to my friend Maya's house. They were such sad, sad train tracks that day, counting shards of green glass bottles, strewn around the chalky earth and rusted rails, the big bushes full of bum clothes. The world was New Year's empty and I was part of the sky, had been up all night and my folks were pissed off at me and I hated them and everything except love and I was alone walking through the relics of winos like there was no world of parents yelling... Man, they yelled all the time, so pissed off, so angry, they were so sad to be around back then. For those moments of rocks crunching beneath my feet in the quiet city, there was no school trying to grade me, no future trying to make me, and it was good, really, I felt deeply good, good sad steps, steps of leaving, going to a friend's, to sit in the incense of her hippie room and think about the new year and then to go through the sad streets, 'cause everything was sad and good that day, sadness opened me up and made me whole. Maya played The Smiths on her car radio and the guitar was sad, *How Soon is Now?* weeping traffic jams into my head. The machine moved the man, and the perfect bomb fell with me down below the freeze, clear eyed sadness laying out over the city, sad as fuck and forever. Maya has a little boy in Prague. I wonder how Solveigh is in Norway, now. The world was a pearl of pure tear drop flower buds blooming in my eyeball full of mercy. Good day, God day, little patch of hard broken bottle train track earth, go on and become a townhouse or a freeway. I still love you and all those that I remember there.

A young woman gets up to get off the bus, going home from work in Century City. She works in a law office, she makes coffee and copies but she just started, not too long ago. She lives in West Los Angeles with roommates, and she writes home and tells them about movies. She goes out and parties on the weekends, just enough to say she wasn't working. She doesn't drive to work, she lives too close to do that. Her parents send her rent money so she can live in the safer part of LA.

She goes home and looks in the mirror. She gets on the computer, does the chatrooms and personals, looking in the mirror all the time. There are no children in her life. There can't be. There is no room. She has told herself. Secretly, she would like to give herself up that way, someday. To have children, to find someone to do that with. Her biology demands it. But there are other things, and child things must wait or not be at all, and with whom? Where do you find people who fit in so many places, who can take care of so many things, who can hold me in so many ways, I mean the ways in which I do not love myself, who could do this for me? Who could hold me that way? A child robs, robs the mother of her life, takes the mother's life and makes it their own. I took my mother's life. I came into her life and took all her things away, her husband became tired, she became tired too. I am in my life now. This is my life. My money, mostly. My time. My phone. Her voice in my ears, telling me not to do what she did. "Don't have yourself." I am going to take a bath, and finish my book, my back aches.

The Mormon Temple horn blower is Silent. Golden, Tall, and Silent.

WESTWOOD BOULEVARD

THE BUS IS MOVING MUCH faster now. Streets are coming up much faster. There are no people waiting to catch it.

Rhino Records, UCLA. I was a Bruin.

Nursery school, Westwood, blamed for everything that went wrong. I didn't do it, I didn't, I wasn't making the curtain move, it was the wind. I swear, to this day, it was the wind. Sure, sonny boy, sure it was, come here and I will beat you with brittle old lady fingers and tickle you with my frosty white hair.

Once I got sick, peanut butter puke, and my dad came to get me and my brother. He came from work, and I loved him so much, he smelt like work, suit and tie and aftershave and a day's worth of office sweat, and all those things smelt like love because he was there getting me because I was sick. It was something for me to see him in his work clothes and work all over him and stepping away from all of that for me. Mom Love was everyday. Dad worked late and came home too tired. Here we were out in the middle of the city, here we were outside and that made it different, he came alone to pick me up, and my brother, not with mom, not at home, it was him, on his own. Out of his downtown office building, the strange world of wearisome honeycombs where they threw calendars on the street on New Years Eve, he came from Spring Street, the Bank of America, came out and got us kids and my little kid sickness, sick feeling like a bug with

138

its guts hanging out, sick, shaky, shivering, weaker than toilet paper, and the old man was there...

Orange Julius car wash, gone wash, was a place to get a burger and a car shine. The bald, winking genie, standing on the rooftop, polishing the cars in the sky, no longer needed, no longer of the moment. Bald car wash genie, where did you go? Stuck in a lamp somewhere, or in a container of Turtle Wax, to be discovered in the consolation prize from *The Price is Right?*

Westwood was the place to go when I was a kid. Everyone went to the movies and hung out there. It was a cool little college village with really cool bookstores and funky shops like the Poster Mat. Man, I got history there. I was eating donuts at Stan's when I was 3 feet tall.

The Eighties will some day be understood. One day the wasted youth Eighties will be known. Not just for Punk Rock, but as the time when kids got crazy in Flock of Seagull polka dots, that's the real news. The Eighties was all about kids freaking out. The kid clubs were all over the city, the new wave disco hip hop culture club cocaine love all around town: Phases, 321, and the mac daddy of them all, The Odyssey. All under age places. Kids roamed the city on these very busses, bummed change at the mall, ate an eggroll, did two lines, smoked a joint. In a world of washed out hippies and lame new age brain deads, the president in a geriatric stupor talking about Star Wars, what the hell was there supposed to be but fantasy? Hardcore fantasy, black became white and white became black and all that mattered was in your pocket, in your love locket, making love in the backseat of some girl's dad's old Cadillac, and the ocean got loud and the sky went on and the ocean played a radio and the sky went on, and the ocean meant it and the sky forgot, and it was all out there in the cliché rain, but I didn't know that it was a cliché, it felt new to me.

Westwood that was where everyone came from all over town, white kids, black kids, Mexicans, but no one had a color, you see, it wasn't like that, not to me, everyone was out inventing themselves into shades of green and purple and blue and shit like that, climbing lysergic rooftops, New Romantic, Mod, Ska, Doctors of Rap, living for the something that has no end, you don't know what end means, you don't know, because you are only 15, 16, and who really knows anyway? Not the old people, not the ones who said they knew when they were kids, but they don't know now, they don't know 'cause if they did... what happened?

But you know it is going to end, that these are the days of fingertip flowers and what you feel is what the world feels and what the world feels is your name, and you don't know anything about the world, you just see down streets and you know them like lost people you used to know in an old school you used to go to and everything you are is in a constant state of never being again, dying, everyday, born again, dead again, with every turn of the page, and you don't care what it looks like, what it sounds like, you just say it, you just are it, looking good in your bad mind, ratty and fantastic, drunk on the sparkly drops that you suck from the air, rooftops full of suicide and sex, you do it all, not thinking, not looking, just rocking on the curb, looking at her, looking at you, listening to a glittering star car stereo. There were break dancers on every corner back then. "Nowhere Girl" played and the fan blew your sweaty ass cool and everyone danced with themselves and everyone was nowhere. It was beautiful nowhere, lost on your first line of glitter, it was a fucked up hair cut and just an endless sky of love, wanting to be wanted louder than the speakers screamed. And it was sad cause no one was anywhere and everywhere you looked it was just kids looking for something bigger than them and better than them and there was nothing and it was beautiful, fantastic, there, get lonely, no girl to talk to, everyone in there cool shoes, trips, sexing in the back room, high lines, hair jelly and gum in the bathroom, one more shot 'cause I love you, you know that it's real 'cause you feel… Give me tonight, then if you don't wanna stay I will forget you… the poetry of love need, the world killer, phantom fantastic, Ziggy Suicide Ocean Plane, you see reality is bullshit, rent is not, but reality is bullshit, you must be able to make yourself into whatever you need to be: why enslave yourself with the reality you were born into but did not choose?

Fly to Hawaii, Mobil Gas, CompuServe, CNN, Merrill-Lynch, DON'T SMOKE, Movies For The Whole Family…

Sepulveda, the longest Street in the city. Probably the longest single street in the world, gotta be the country. From the north tip of the San Fernando valley all the way down through the Santa Monica Mountains all the way across West LA to the airport and on through the South Bay and into Long Beach. I don't even know where the thing ends. It's an old trail. Traveled for hundreds, maybe thousands of years. All the big streets and freeways follow the old natural ways. Figueroa and the 110. Olympic and the 10, San Fernando Road and the 5, Temple and the 101, all these corridors fit into the land, following creeks and rivers, cutting through mountains at their isthmus, just like Sepulveda does here. Named for a Mexican ranch owner who died poor, I believe. His property tax too much to maintain in the USA.

The 405 underpass, there are no people walking around here. None. The emptiness covers you with full lit big commuter streets full of cars waiting to go and those going, metal grim faces and the sidewalks are empty, I mean really empty out here, Hollywood seems like an ant farm compared to this. The tall glass walls of offices sit on the street, little patch of grass at the entrance... Why bother? The glass walls reflect the lights of traffic, red, yellow and green, the cars too, upside down, cars down the street until the cars look small, a river, a stuck river of shiny metal teeth. Sepulveda is full, the freeway is full, and here is a bum in the middle of the street, a man with a cup out for change, his head is down, eyes peering into the glassy eyes and windows, the office people, the traffic people, some man in his car, eyes red with a days worth of air-conditioning and paper moving. What the hell does he do all day? Whatever it is he doesn't want to see this man, this man who brings his trouble right to his window. Isn't there some other way?

His gray figure walking like an apparition of exhaust and desert dust, rattling a cup like a character from a Victorian poverty book, but the setting is science fiction, he is a cyber vagrant, destitute on the set of Logan's Run.

The cars ignore him. In one version of the story he has shoes, but I am not seeing that one. In the other he has no shoes and his feet are bleeding, he is worse than Christ with his bloody feet. Someone calls 911 on their cell phone and somehow convinces them a man is dying in the street. Paramedics come to help the man who is dying from the feet. They take him to their ambulance and he says, "Don't touch my feet. I finally have them just right."

"They're infected. You are gonna loose your foot."

"You don't understand. This is the way it has to be. This is the way the world is. There must be dead people walking through the fields of traffic. I must bleed on this world. I must keep it alive."

The medics leave to go eat somewhere.

Fade back: the man is small, down the street, wading into the headlights, breathing the exhaust. The bus gets a green light and we move on.

Two bum ladies talk in the back seat.

The vagrant lunatics are insane. They have no separation between inner and outer toilet bowl worlds. They cannot keep their shit in the bowl. They don't even make it into the bathroom. They stink. But be generous, man, mad asphalt gods have taken over the planet and we all go on and try to make our biology work as if everything was normal and natural, but the nut case street psychos don't do this. It is as if they grow from the asphalt to scream and beg on corners. They are the voice made of all things that this world has to offer, bats in their eyes, the light of razor blade suns in their mouths, crazed fountains of spilt psychosis. They have no choice. They scream about the winged phantoms of mechanical lust, the dead mothers you didn't kiss goodbye, predators and fathers, alien mind-control brigades, media barons, the sadistic football players, heinous cheerleaders or their own drug pumped disease.

Garbage in the gutter, cars on the roads, clean sidewalks, the night is full on, some folks have gotten on the bus, our life is a taut cord, held in the light, pluck it, its tone is the pulse of an ocean that goes beyond these points. We have killed a lot of things trying not to die, but look deeply, look close, into the sub stratum of super existence, look into the labyrinth world of concrete streets and steel, because this is where we live, look and you will see something, something that is not controlled, it is no mere ghost, nor phantom exiled to the pistons, or dream dropped onto the microprocessor, but rather a misshapen creature with weedy flowers where there should be eyes, the color of blood, the trail of their excrement is the red color of the hills, mortar fire on the city streets, and in these eyes you see the streets burn, the rage, the fear comes from within, the bomb that will explode lives within us, explodes within us, all of us.

The earth turns with fire at its core, hell keeps us doing right, fire is our knowledge, is our gun, is our bowl of soup, is our life of bombs and addictions, is our good time, is our music, is in every word that we have ever written, lamp lit at night in the dark cloister of the monk, the scribe, penning the verses of fire, the burning wheel, the chariot of hallelujah roses, to burn is true, to rage is right, we must praise the fire, fire tore at the primal body and gave us the voices of the gods, the hands of the makers, the feet of servants, the heart of heaven, our genius is the blaze, the Promethean curse, the fact of the fire is that things must burn and where the essence of fire, the knowledge, the power of self and soul, where that is denied the physical flames will fan harder, tearing at more than buildings, tearing at the emptiness which has turned these streets and walls into a mad place, and what you have when it is done is ashes and nothing.

Oh, hear me sons of Uniroyal, children of the off ramp, what is Holy in a land where no one knows the name of his neighbor, where no one knows the eyes of those who came before? Who are the voices that we hear in the weeds in the dream of traffic America that we are all born into and out of, the dream of reflections, the dream of terror, the dream of grief, the dream of loneliness, the dream of time, and the dream of no time... this is the dream and how the dream walks.

You know what I think? I think people just give up their humanity the first shot they get, step right into the styrofoam light. This is the way it should be. Why bother being human, vulnerable, out of it? Why risk humiliation by feeling something, by loving something, someone, you will only lose?

You know this gangster death trip, it is holding us all back.

You know the cop death trip, holding us back, to let go the fear of dying. No, it is the fear of living. Death is certain, life is not. That is what they say in the army. That is what they teach the peach recruits. Where did I hear that? At Church Street station in San Francisco, a bit high, a coffee shop full of freaks and my kind self getting some food for a homeless lady. What the fuck, that is crazy, what was I into? That's cool, but this jar head kid is in their getting french fries and this old dyke, drunk, eating coffee, gets off on this guy because the Navy had just blown up a plane full of Islamic pilgrims. And he said this, "Death is certain, life is not: the code of the military." That is what they teach in the world. Who knows how to live. Nobody knows how to make a life that matters. Maybe one or two people, okay maybe more, okay a bunch of people, but they got lucky, they found it in some hidden little bottle that washed up on the sand. Most people don't have a clue what they are supposed to do with their lives. Shopping is about the only thing that people are given to do. The poor people can't even do that. The human real, the real human, the needs, real needs human, the real human needs to do something more than buy things.

We are our needs, we are not ideas or some measured bit of putty floating around the ceiling of some store, we cannot buy ourselves, we cannot read ourselves, we cannot compose ourselves, we are bodies, fucking, killing when we can't get high enough to forget and dying when we can. We are fucked. You might be okay. But we are fucked.

My family never belonged in Santa Monica. We were crazier than anyone else I knew. When you grow up in the Los Angeles you can be from anywhere you want. You are from anywhere. All worlds are available here, 'cause when I was a kid I didn't feel like I was from anywhere but myself and my crazy family. My great grandmother came to the west in a covered wagon, homesteaded in Spokane, Washington, my grandfather built Nazarene churches all over Los Angeles, I got a cousin in prison for murder and the rest have gone insane, so I felt a deeper, different kind of white than most people I knew in Santa Monica.

As a kid, midday Shick Center commercials would make me sad, "Don't take the car, you'll kill yourself."

Those commercials spoke to me. I saw this one thing on TV about a drunk-as-hell postal employee who would go on these 5 day underwear drunk binges. The wrecked life. That felt like something I could understand.

But you were popular, Steve, you had friends, you got sex, you were on the team.

Yes, true. Crazy. What can I say? I think of Cat, my wife, holding Penelope after she was born, how they were something strange and beautiful, a terrible creature of wonderful truth, and I, a person thinking the world to be clearly insane, life to be a strange and worrisome trial, helped make it, made life, enacted it, let it come through me, life is not the bad thing, life is the wonder eyes thing, it is the blessing, something else is the trouble. Here I was a parent. I had gone and become nothing but sight, look- ing at stuff that only blind people see, not the sight of eyes, but the sight of blood, the sight of water, the sight of death, the sight of living, the sight of sound, the sight of hearts, the sight of seeing, the sight of being and not being, the sight of knowing and not knowing.

I am amazed, and this is a crime, a crime because when you are amazed you are weak, and vulnerable, there is a hot air balloon of vision up your ass, it hurts like loving love without a lover near, death to reasons, don't make no sense, amazement runs through you, you cannot deny it, or anything that it touches, it is alive, alive, vital, "Vita,

Vida, Vegamina," drawing breath, as it draws a circle around you and one for each person we love, that is what we all do. Here we are drawing circles onto the paper, into the ocean, lookin' up to see what grade we got, but no, there's none of that here, no grades, only 29 million flavors of time, wounded streets, a world of tangled sunlight, on a clear day you can see yourself... statues and fingernails, tentacles of eyeball strings seeing all the worlds of spring and harm, music and wounds, wounds because we live open, open, that is how it really is.

I won't die stupid without my own mind, groveling for some dignity. Fuck 'em who think reality is something that you don't feel, something not beautiful, something that doesn't touch, who believe vulnerability is a liability.

Nuart Theatre, there it goes, saw a million movies there but I can't think of what they were, all I can think of is James Dean, yelling, "I got the Bullets, I got the Bullets," in *Rebel Without A Cause*. I must have seen that movie ten times, all of them at the Nuart and the Fox Venice.

James Dean, freaky man/boy, bent wanter of lilies and flight, a weed, a bone, a Jazz City Saxophone, something to be, hurt heart life cigarette lover, spitting Shakespeare at the palm trees of free city sorrow.

You think I care about what he really was, or what his movies really are? For me, at that time it was a ticket into myself, to ride the steel clouds in a world made of plastic to-go cartons. To me he was cool, completely and totally. Good looking for the right reasons. I was sick with it, went out and bought a James Dean jacket from the same place the studios purchased his in 1954, a fact acquired from research in the periodical section of the Santa Monica Public Library. The clothing store was Matson's in Hollywood, the corner of Wilcox and Hollywood Blvd. The salesman, a real Hollywood prime rib swinger gone gray... it must have been 1981. Everything was over, all scenes at hot spots gone cool, but this guy was there, so beautiful with a gold watch and a gray turtleneck, selling men's apparel on Wilcox, told me, with such tender sincerity, so kind 'cause I was just a kid, told me it was the same jacket, exactly, that had been used in *Rebel*. The same. It was red. It was too big. I didn't care, I bought it anyway. Right now I am gonna cry thinking: how beautiful it was that the gray haired clothier would tell me, insist, that I was buying the very same make as Dean wore 30 years before...

Dolores Coffee Shop, big red letters in the air, against a dark sky of orange halos and plane lights in nighttime smog, DOLORES across the sky. There is a high school kid writing verse at the counter. There is a bent city monk reciting litanies of his own design. Papa Bach Bookstore ghost cats, jumping over the books. I think of Tony Russo, AKA, A.P. Russo, the guy was a voice in the early Seventies poetry scene, definitely happening, pals with Bukowski, but far freakier. Then he just said fuck it and quit the scene, just worked selling books at Chatteron's and being a scholar of his own mind and universe. In the early Nineties, he left LA and ended up in Nebraska, where he dies with his lungs buried in Cancer, his words buried in Cancer. He was cool to me, leaning on my shoulder, drunk in Ye Rustic Inn quoting Blake's "The Sick Rose." "The world is sick, man, it's the worm, eating the rose, Steve." Tony Russo, your unseen pages hang from the sky.

There is something ecstatically, drearily alcoholic about these few blocks, perhaps it is the Veteran's Hospital down the street, or the Mini Civic Center and Jail, Agent Orange brother babbling beneath a pile of leaves in front of the Courthouse, sad Samuel waiting for the bus to lock up a love deal gone bad, scolding the cold front, "Fear, man, fear," I got the fear, sit up straight and you can hear, you can hear me if you sit up straight.

Every time I pass this place, I sense old men in corduroy suit coats with poetic intentions of building a secret structure of words that would hold the sunlight of bright November hangover skies. I feel them, lining up for Shakespeare at the Royal, needing the words of the Bard to push them through the words of these streets and the streets that they see in their lovely furthest coast need, Los Angeles, a desolate aesthetic of weary finality. I saw them, these men with the vapor of heavy thought hangovers, Academies of the Individual Mind built outside the walls of the University, scholars of the burger joint, bus bench across town with hashish visions of Concerto, Apocalypse, Orgasm, Darkest Sky, Birth, whatever makes it. I see them growing weed style from a salty finger of the winter life in this dandelion sun... gone town.

Papa Bach, MacBeth on a blue bus, bum life holy wanter, I got the call, was inspired, told to do this. Shakespeare did it. All those freaks murdering and lying and doing anything to get that real love. Why did we go and see all of those Shakespeare films? They were hard for me and my brother to sit through. We always checked the minutes on the film to see what we were getting into. They were long, *Othello* with Lawrence Olivier was like three hours and *Hamlet* more, and *MacBeth* with Orson Welles was so dark and strange you didn't know what was happening half the time. But it was good. It was a good thing to be made to do. Our father used his power well. It was cool to know where all the clichés and weird witches came from and hell, we did what the old man wanted. He was a strong man who got deeply upset with things. You didn't want that to happen. So Shakespeare on Saturday mornings it was. Everyone should be forced to see the Bard's works. It is good for the whole family. You get to see how being fucked up is a classic virtue of western culture.

Behind the Post Office there is the mural of California after the BIG ONE, the earthquake of judgment, the state fallen off into the sea, a freeway broken, like a torn jaw, hanging out over the waves, the myth of the final western roads that carry the weight of all manner of haunted Jerusalem futures. The whole continent leans toward us and the world leans to this continent, Los Angeles holds the weight of the world's need for destruction, the city cracks and falls the million miles that something must fall when it is a dream. The jaws of sin surround our houses and our sidewalks. Oh, Canine of Lost Long Love, you will pay for the murder of my people, you will pay for the demise of Holy Time, feel this molten fear of the Lord. You can smell the ocean salt in the air.

Used to be Arlene's Donuts at Bundy, used to be. All night. Used to be Daddy's Burritos. 24 Hours. Now, Starbucks. Hey, they tore down the Tom's No. 5. I puked there. It's gone. The bus drives.

Shakey's, Ski Haus, Jerry's Liquor, mom and pop bottles of rum, little boys in the backseat back from Sunday School, we'd be drinking and screaming Sunday to the ceiling of our need. Don't fuck with me, baby... Sunday School, you know, I went to a lot of Sunday School. You know what I remember from Sunday School? Driving crosstown, from Santa Monica out to Hollywood and Gower, I recall prostitutes, hookers, Sunset Blvd. ladies, standing in the 8 am Sunday, beneath an All-American Burger tree, yellow jumpsuit, open with a large brown breast showing shining in my little boy eye... mouth open staring out the window... "What's that?" No need for explanation, blood knew, my blood knew.

The Lord loves us and asks us things we would rather not have to answer, do you want me now, do you know that I am as alone as you, do you know that I have the same dream as you and I can not find the real? And the dream says, "You can fuck, fuck and fall or make a family and love."

20TH STREET

St. John's Hospital at 20th street in Santa Monica. The sky is fresh dark with blue eyes. I was born in this hospital, and worked there when I was 18, just before I went to college. This is where the first notes for the first poems came from. Ah yes, something deeply mad, I know not what it is called, or where it has been, but it is an ancient thing, the thing that bit my ass and made me bleed words, bleed words, I kid you not, that is how it fucking was and now, it's just blood and words all over the place. What is blood? What is a word? What is this ancient thing I am always talking about?

Crazy to roll by there, thinking, born there, thinking: BORN, all is born, and I was born, and my wife, and we made some more born and then there are other borns that happen every moment, every moment is a born and died thing, a street comes to you, breaking out of the exhaust, faces come to you the same, Pound's apparitions on the Metro, and they leave, go away, and you are covered with their afterbirth tadpole aroma, and born is what? Becoming something, coming into somewhere, being but not knowing, like an infant, alien shaped things, bodies of pure alive, no now or then, just blood in the arteries and back down through the veins, just, not even, not even that, more, you are a body, but a body of air and the single need to breathe in this new place you have come to, keep this body alive, you are born and you are the base pulp of

153

everything that surrounds you, the magma heartbeat at the center of the steel sea, new life, breathing big deal and a so what, new universe of human soul, holding that new-ness, without knowing it, but knowing and touching the newness of themselves, the new walls that will go around them and make them protect their lives and living place in a way that they had not before, the new ocean that is the baby breaking new ground inside the parents, new conti-nents for the baby sea to splash and torrent onto, the shore that the water will shape, and what is not strong will fall, what is not necessary will fall, what is not you will fall, what is not being will fail and if you don't let it fall it will destroy you.

Up all night with a child crying is so hard to hear, "Please stop crying, please stop, shut up the crying." Life doesn't let you cry this much, you gotta stop the crying, think about that: why does the baby crying hurt so much? Just cause you can't watch the basketball game? No, of course not. It is tearing at you, taking you there, to where you hurt, yes, you can hear them yelling at you, "Stop cry-ing! Goddamn it!" And I have said the same thing. It is sad. I am sorry, little girls of mine.

Oh, little girls of mine, so beautiful and full of your own life. I am sorry I get mad and Penelope tells me, "No! No getting mad. Time-out for you!!" It is so sweet and cute and sad that I want to die. I want to stop getting mad and play Candyland with Maya and Penelope.

I see my anger, my rage, coming from my life with my folks, I really see it. I am not blaming or pissing, just see-ing. I can see me little and them, my folks, freaking out and I can feel it coming into me, lodging in my tissue, fragile place of eternal hummingbird bones. The baby crying in the middle of the night is a cry in the middle of my psychic marrow, disturbing hulls sunken, encrusted, barnacled, buried, something sediment, something so primary it may not even be from my own time alive, but passed down to me in the darkest sub-aqueous matter of the chromosome forest, eyes of fire from the marine graves of ships that sailed through carbonless nebulas of the first novas, I swear, I am open in a place that I cannot stay open, and be bombarded with the square circles of concern, the infant creature comes from a different place, and so do we all, so do we all.

There is a hole in our head when we are born, a fontanel, and it doesn't go away until we are quite old, not totally away, it fills with dust and things of traffic and what you have to walk through to keep the food coming and all that, but you never lose it, the wound, and we talk about the wind, or the hole, the open piece of head, without even knowing it. We talk about the tenor of the wind, the velocity of momentary nations, and the Jehovah rose bee kisses that fall all around us.

We are open. If we close, what will we need the emptiness for? What will we sing about?

The night is dark and light pricks its flesh only in places, words are shadows, we see in darkness, the universe is desire, formed in a place where the heat bent, a crack in the purity of the flame and in that our atom was forged, we ride on the light that carved our shadows, into the never was. We empty our souls and breathe the water that is without end, without answer. Oh, Lord, oh Gravitational Pull, holy force much like a Whirlpool washing machine, kill all the killing that we hold in our selves, trying to see ourselves in mirrors that cannot see. Water that shimmers across your hand, a web of silence that composes you in seashells and garbage cans, tangling into a sleeping train of genius snakes lusting through the sea of seeds that I hold in this finger pointing at my shoes.

I need to get drunk, I need to get mad, argue, masturbate to the heavens, write a poem, create an airplane of Q-Tips and plastic forks, make a backyard wall, mosaiced with mirrors and glass buttons, get the car and drive home and be hungry and try not to bug Cathy with all of this, but who am I kidding?

Life is a dog just walking around looking for something, anything, sniff sniff, the world tells you what do to, life doesn't have directions, life doesn't have goals, life moves around, living, exploding in genesis moments, of fire cracker bones and fish from a Novaed sea, memory, sex all over the passengers and passerby, in life you die a million times just crossing the street, and you are born a million more with every moon that rings its orbit looking for water. You are stars full of bombs, bombs full of eyes, eyes full of lips, lips filled with exit signs from another time and a sea of hands, a sea that spills fingers from the wall all around our neon soledad, sparkling Nazarene seaweed. A hand is a day of long song Clifford Brown horns and numberless clocks, clocks that count out loud, the alphabet of volcanoes, spewing peacock feather gasoline, exploding shells of Butterfly Sun.

Oh, let's all kiss the wheels of roses and worms on which we hang and no one, not even Sylvia Brown, really knows why, but there is a why all by its lonesome in the

way we breathe, in the way love is truly loved, so deep
inside you all fall apart, stop breathing, come, come, come
and cry because your wings have been touched by the
wings of the eternal temporal human thing essence deal
down deep, yes, touched in the deepest hummingbird
fuck, your lungs become a bag of wings, and if she ain't
pregnant after that get checked out by a doctor 'cause the
infant said, "Yes," spoke sweet single notes from a star
coming down, spoke "Yes," little sack of bones and belly
walk through this world, Penelope, Maya, our notes of
sun upon the night, upright, cradled, shaped by the
vaporous hands of what it is that surrounds us, that is us.

I have two kids. Amazing. Now I am the one with mul-
tiple boxes of cereal. I am the one signing my girls up for
gymnastics class. I go to the arts and crafts table at the
Fair and cut and paste with them. I am the one with the
kids in the backseat. I am the one with a wife who works
her ass off bringing them up right, love right, up at night
and gotta listen to them yelling all day. Cat, you and me
have made people. Now I get the blame for whatever happens. All fear comes back to me.

I was 18 when I worked at this hospital. I felt holy and
insane just being around the sick, the dying, the being
born, and those giving birth, it wasn't about car crashes
and gunshot victims at Saint John's. You had to have
insurance to even use toilet paper in the place. It was
about people, mostly older, frail and dying, scared of the
walls and the beds, everything, me, the doctors, the nurs-
es, people, old ladies asking us to make sure their pets
were alright. This one lady, crying about her Siamese cat,

I swear to god she had crossed eyes just like a Siamese cat, herself. It was too much. I couldn't believe it. I felt like an egg made of dried hair pushing her gurney down the hall. "Sure, sure, I'll make sure your cat's okay." Or the old lady, when I lifted her from the bed to the gurney to go get x-rays, she was so tiny and frail, her hips fit in my hand. People were naked of themselves. They were dying and their entire lives and you know what I mean when I say life, the whole thing, hung around them, came from them, sat on them, like it does, I guess, but I had never seen it do that before. What the fuck did I know? I thought I knew something. I read *The Razor's Edge*. But an old lady frail in your hands is a whole other deal.

Death. I met Death there. It was a very low key meeting, but serious, let me assure you. I only took a few dead people down to the morgue. Okay, it's not like I was doing battlefield KP in Vietnam, that was done by a bus driver I rode with in Junior High, Mr. Handy. He wouldn't tell us about it, said it was too horrible for kids to know about what happened to enemy genitalia in a war. Mr. Handy. Damn.

It wasn't the city morgue, but so what, the deal was the first time I went to get a body, I took it all to heart. I let it all in. It was very heavy. The dispatcher called me, said there's a morgue call, you have to do it. So I am sent with this older woman, 65, an Argentine Jew who speaks Yiddish and Spanish. She was very serious about the whole thing. You couldn't be foolish with her on a morgue call, no jokes, no bullshit. It was all solemn and ceremonial. Everything, how you put the gloves on, how she took the big brass morgue key ring from its special place, to the kind of cart you used. A morgue call was done with a special gurney, that looked a lot like a coffin. It was all very intense, you were carrying the dead along the way to their final resting place and it was done with respect. Fanny was her name, Safardic Jew from Buenos Aires. Old but fit and right on. I did like she said.

Everything was all still as we went down the hall, early in the day, and everyone who was working knew what the special hooded cart meant. Like I said, it looked like a coffin. It was a cart fully covered with a black vinyl shell. Everyone you passed nodded, or looked away or looked down or smiled weird at you 'cause they knew someone on one of the floors didn't make it. It didn't work, whatever had been tried. There was a dead person in the hospital and Fanny and I had to get the body.

When we got to the dead room it was all quiet and I was thinking the whole time that I am going to pick up a dead old lady who had died in her sleep. 86 years alive. Will I see her face, and I am gonna scream? Is it gonna look like my grandma? Will her eyes be open? What am I going to see?

We got in the room, everything was still, the dust had the calm eyes of death. Eyes like a loved one looking down over the departed. Death, the end, not a killer, not a ghost, just death, just there, just doing its job. It was horrible. There was no room for choice in those death eyes, no justice, or remorse, or anything that living people live for. All I saw were eyes filled with what must have been love from the Other Side. And the body was there, wrapped up in a plastic trash bag. That's it. 86 years in a white Glad bag. I was disappointed, that I didn't get to look at the dead lady's face, but really I was glad, because I didn't want to see her face… full of what she was saying, thinking, dreaming when death unlocked the door and sat down next to her.

So you got to get the dead person onto the special hooded cart. How do you do it? You got to pick the dead person up. Dead people are heavy. Since I was me, I got to pick up the torso and head of the old lady. My partner, Fanny, she kind of lifted the feet onto the cart. I had to hug my end of the body. I had no idea how heavy it would be and how delicate I should be. I had never held a dead person before. I got my arms around the trash bag and lifted. She was dead, and heavy as hell. She was slipped from my grip. Fanny got freaky for a moment, held up her hands to say, "What are you doing? Take care with the dead! Fool!" I felt bad. I hugged the dead lady tighter, trying to get a better grip, trash bag dead body in my face, smelling sick smell of death all up my nose, gooey dead flesh beneath the plastic film of the bag.

I thought of my folks. I thought of them asking, "How was your day at work?"

"Oh, you know, strained my back embracing the flesh of death. What about you?"

Hands hugging dead body flesh. I didn't know about dead people. They were still people for the most part, they just weren't alive. I didn't know what they could feel. I just did what Fanny said, trying not to hurt anything. I got my end of the body onto the cart. The head lolled around. I felt for her nose, to make sure she was face up. Procedure. If the body is face down the blood settles in the face and wrecks it, making open caskets very uncomfortable if not impossible.

We walked with the cart of the dead, to the elevator and down into the basement, to the morgue, a room with an autopsy slab, and two big walk-in refrigerator lockers, we opened the refrigerator door, wheeled the body in, shut the door. End of morgue call. Take the brass ringed key back to its nail.

Right On. You live a hundred years, ride elevators of joy and despair, make families, make dreams, lose love and loved ones, live through wars, depressions, bombs, atomic explosions and revolutions, holocausts, society exploding psychic tear gas, knitting mittens and kissing your children, live and then die and your body gets wrapped in plastic and some kid 4 months out of high school is pinching your nose, making sure your face doesn't get smashed on the gurney, which in fact did happen to Bob Barker's wife, and it destroyed her face.

There you are holding the bag someone's life came and went in your hands: still born babies, 86 year old grandmothers, each and all going down to the big refrigerators in the basement, and there wait for the proper ceremony of their people and be laid to rest. Until then, though, they were just dead bodies in a cooler and no one was there.

There was this one guy there who went to my high school. He was a rock and roll guy, failed classes, smoked pot. He took me on my second morgue call. He loved morgue calls. He requested them. He also dug Post-Operation calls. With him, there was no ceremony, you got the key and pushed the cart, put the gloves on 'cause you didn't want dead person fungus on your hands. We went into the room, each got an end, counted three, picked up the body and threw it onto the cart. Just picked it up and threw the thing, dead slab of meat that it was, and he said, "It's dead. It doesn't hurt it. Don't worry." A light bulb turned on! Of course, it didn't hurt. The gravity I felt with Fanny seemed absurd now.

This guy was into it in a whole different way. It was heavy for him, but it wasn't about a life ending and all that. It was something else. "Wanna see something," he asked, lifting up the lid of a refrigerator. "Check this out! You ever see this before?" And he was holding up some poor soul's leg, frozen, wrapped in plastic, strictly butcher shop. Then he showed me where the arms were kept and the hearts, and then onto the wall of shelves where the eyes were kept in little jars, a wall of eyeballs in science fluid staring at you. I didn't say anything. He started singing, "Eyes without a face, you got no human race." A Billy Idol song popular at the time. I laughed. It was cool. Meat. That's it. Let's sing: "My Grandma's Leg/is in the deep freeze./The doctors are picking at her varicose veins."

The voice in the ceiling comes on: "Listen. It is all so important because finally it does not matter. Listen. That is why it is important, it is important because it will not matter, finally, you just stop working and you go and they pinch your nose and cut your hand off and look at it under a microscope. And that's it."

I wonder, myself, what happens to sight? I do not believe that we lose it. How can we stop seeing? I mean, like with blind people—they don't see the world, but they do see. They see something. What do the dead see? Why did they name that lake the Dead Sea? In music is there such a thing as a dead "C?" The dead see you shoplifting their clothes. The morgue, at night, or when no one's there, some dead guy comes out, a ghost, a flame, a door, and looks at his old eyeballs sitting on the shelf and laughs.

Birth and Death, they're everywhere.

Santa Monica: my boyhood, lovely sand and sea time, your rents are too high. Santa Monica: the ocean there, shimmering at the end of the street, the Pacific Ocean Motherfucker, the Atom Bomb oh, oh… very nice, walking in the sun, huge freakin' waves tore down the pier, that was sad. On the old pier, I caught lots of fish when I was a kid, old bait store and hot dog joints. The new pier is not the same, not in my mind. Eziekel from the Bible fished at my pier, hippies and gods, old salty fisherman pier bums, one said, "Come with me, I got something for you." My mom thought, "What the hell?" She came with me and the old man rummaged through his junk stuffed van, rummaged and dug and pulled out a fishing pole, little white pole and simple reel, my first pole, before that only fishing with a drop line, good only for catching star fish. So I got a pole, a gift from a whitebearded beachcomber pier man. Where did he go, where did the biblical bums of the beach bohemia go?

What is Cathy doing now? Playing with Penelope, feeding Maya, feeding the cats. No, no way, she hates the cats. I am rooted. Yes, a plant stuck in the ground, with leaves of family all around me.

Americans are dropping bombs on people and their families right now.

Cosmic commuter memory headlights break into a billion slivered directions, all the worlds of spring and harm. It is easier to just go straight and get the car and go home, but they are in me, and I must go down them, always, like inert gasses, these memories, ideas, diagrams, they sit stoic and potent, waiting for the right partner in the right heat in the right angle, with the right amount of light, and the right smell, and then they all begin blooming.

These cosmic dew drops from your very own eternity, you know the things I am talking about, dense flesh walls of the real, the now, invisible liquid of eyes that see in all manner of light, it is all over me, filling the seat of this bus with a strange brine, water rising in billows, torrents and currents, accept it or drown in a panic, the water rises, covers the seats, an old man sleeping with a newspaper, he rubs his nose, the garbage floats on the top of the water, the bus driver with a snorkel, windshield wipers on the inside of the bus, crabs walking over the gum stuck to the floor and a halibut sits down beside me and looks me up and down with the two flat eyes on the same side of its head, says something, and swims away as other fish and crabs and soda pop cans come up and lay their debris on my body, and give me fortune cookie sayings of useful wisdom.

I don't understand any of it, it is fish talk, the water pours out into the street, floods the asphalt and storm drains, destroys gas stations, igniting geysers of fire, cars are lifted in torrents, apartment walls crack, then fall. The street is full of debris, teeth, lips, limbs, and shoes swirl among other indecipherable garbage. For what, I ask, is this pandemonium? There is no answer.

The water rises and takes all with it, freeways, houses, people in bed fornicating, their sex uninterrupted by the tide, they continue, they turn around and begin the dog, the man is captain of the bed, the woman watches what is coming, they are going strong. It is me doing it. It is me and my wife, doing it in the middle of the worst flood of memory that Santa Monica has ever seen, HELL YEAH! She kisses me and swims away, I lay on top of the car like some kind of Prometheus who hasn't stolen anything. I am descended upon by something mermalian and butterfly, my wife again, this time she has brought a friend, her other self? Alter ego? Goddamn, it's too hot! Oooh, I can't take it. I'm going to explode.

We begin our copulation again, on top the floating car, the copulation takes us through the steel forests of the concrete river, the crumbled warehouse walls of once proud industry, lakes of pig's blood, spilt to feed a needless need, we go down through the last willows of a forgotten swamps, secrets beneath the streets, and the sky turns purple then cracks open with illuminated streaks of perspiration, pornographic teardrop tracks of erosion in the surface of cement, I can see close into her skin, I roll over holding her, bone deep wrenching of tearful thing drops, want to say like muscles being torn in abyssal caverns, recipes for disease and cure bubbling up.

We sleep, not we of these bones, but we of the language of feathers and bubbles and bells and traffic, in language like ocean waves crashing and rolling up onto the shore, and back down and sand crabs spill down into the sea, I am naked on the floor, my mom walks in on me, she is tired, I am seventeen, "Jacking off again?" My wife's voice comes to me, "You better not fuck around on me. I'll kill you if you fuck around on me." It is love.

"What? Are you thinking about fucking again? It's been nothing but fuckin' and freakin' all the way across town." It is my grandmother, she has been dead for five years, her voice has changed, she sounds really Country and Jewish, must be in heaven, with Yahweh, and all this is like being five again and seeing your parents naked and fucking, hearing the strange voices that they make, the voices that are not them, twisted into a strong love of nipples and eyeballs being given to the sun, and little boy me, there I am knocking on the door, "Hey, what's going on in there? Hey, I'm hungry," and they nakedly open the door and nicely tell me to hold on, they are talking… I saw my mom naked.

Later, in first grade, I made a little magazine, construction paper and marker, all I drew were big breasted ladies. The bus moves and the streets pass and the water rises and the mermaids flip me off. I must be going down. In fact, I have drowned with lungs full of ovarian sunshine.

I am seeing fish on the floor here.

"I was born," scream the fish. "Know me," scream the fish. "I was born and my eyes made sense. You, Sir Steve, have made another born, you pushed the button, go forth, we are proud of you, you have chosen to do it, thou hath made life in the strange land… Good, we say. Sure, cut out the coupons, do comparison shopping, too bad you can't do drugs occasionally, but you can't. Talk about basketball, sweat, get mad, because you are mad, and know, never forget, the water covers everything."

Thus spake the fish on the bus.

The bus stops and picks up a man. He, too, is leaking his ocean onto the seats.

There was a little neighborhood market near here, around the corner. We would go there to get our candy before we went to the movies. It was cheaper. The store belonged to a little old lady. In my memory it was a candy store mostly, a clapboard corner store with an apartment on top, and big pepper trees draping over its top. A family lived on top. When you walked in the door jingled your entrance. It was dark in there, not much light, it felt like the candy was better because you couldn't see so good in the place. She stood in the back, thin woman in a dress, with wire rim glasses and dark hair pulled back. She stood in the cool shadows over the counter with the candy and the ice cream. "Right over there," she'd point to the M&Ms. I used to think she was so old she musta been born in 1901.

Len Sheridan Toyota Car Lot. What happened to the Chevrolet lots? I rode my bike around here. Rolled tires into the street. Me and my brother went to the movies every weekend, all the time, to the Criterion, the Cinema, the Monica Twins. My brother, Jerry, and I, in there for hours and hours, we'd see movies three times straight, crawl on the floor, look for money, once I scavenged all the pop corn buckets, took them home and built me a robot.

We saw stuff like *The Strongest Man in the World*, *GO FOR IT*, *The Buddy Holly Story*. I really loved the Buddy Holly Story, he was Goddamn cool. I walked home singing at the top of my lungs "ALL-A MA LOVE, ALL-A MA KISSIN', YOU DON'T KNOW WHAT YOU

BEEN A-MISSIN', OH BOY." I was like 10 years old.

American Hotwax, I loved that one. Rock and Roll was in my soul. Chuck Berry played for free. It was the story of Allen Freed and the exploding rock and roll revolution of the American Kid Soul. I started riding my bike with my red denim jacket.

Oh, the films, wall sized images, a cave full of sound, consumed me. I was enveloped, wombed, then spit out, weekly, eye exploded, mind as big as the dark, to the ceiling, as big as a wall and all over the dark rows of big eyed kids, the world was far away and we all were alone, we didn't even know each other, all the kids in the movie theatre, bound by the shimmering darkness, kids in the movie theatre, left to watch movies about Big Foot and UFOs, *Spiders from Space Attack the Trailer Park*, *Towering Inferno*, Monty Python's *Holy Grail*? Nah, they wouldn't let us in for that, rated R.

It always felt weird to come out into the afternoon, thinking, "What to do now?" The old ladies feeding their friends, the pigeons. The ocean was there, pinball at the pier, let's go collect cans, sit in the sand, let's go to Jack in the Box, Angels watch the children as they grow… The bird of roses scavenges your bones to build a nest for you or something… I don't really know.

The movie that stays in my head, I don't know the name. A Carolina trash family, ten people or so, turn to crime, and they run, doing crime all over the countryside, at the end they visit their old grandmamma who is sick, at a quiet country house party, but they have been set up, the cops know they are there and ambush them. They die in a bloody and tragic, glorious gun battle with the police.

They were doomed people. I loved them. I was sad for them. I knew they would not get away. I hoped there was some place they could run. I imagined a place, a turn, a state, far away, a hideout, a different sphere, dimension, an idea, justice, God, that God would see them and their suffering and step in make things clear and right. But there was no place or answer or help and we all knew it. I forget all the details but I know and knew then, they were looking for love, crucifixion love, wordless freedom, heaven style, to escape the fate of being soul crushed poverty broken human beings, they wanted the sunshine... a blood soaked sun is better than none.

My brother and I went home. We knew home was fucked as we came to the door. It smelled of incense and cigarettes and alcohol, which always meant the same sad and drunk things. Sorry am I that I think this here, standing with my brother, viewing the body of our father, drunk, passed out, stoned beyond eyesight, babbling vomit stained mouth, I mean, gone. The house broken up, mom hiding in the closet, what the fuck is this? What the hell were you doing? Why'd you want us to see you like that? Was there some message in your rage? Were you trying to teach me about life and pain? You knew we were coming home, motherfucker. Why'd I have to live your nightmare? Then you tell me when I'm having my kid that being a parent is shaping a soul, so you knew, you knew, and you did it all anyway. Fuck you, Holy Man.

I split. Left. Went. Was Gone. 8 years old. That was it. Museums and all the other shit they showed me, cool, but I made a note to myself right there, to always have a place in my pocket that I could stay. I threw on my cool Levi jacket, hopped on my dirt bike, went down to the closed down car lot and popped wheelies over the weeds growing up between the cracks of asphalt. I was an outlaw, without a home, hungry for sunshine and meaning. Rock and roll oldies playing in my storming mind.

Where did Jerry go? Where was my brother. I don't know? I bailed and got deep by myself. That has been the story of our relationship. I think he stayed in the house, or he sat out on the sidewalk in front of the apartments, all alone and cried where no one saw and no one sees. Sad as hell. Sad as hell. I had the bike and the jacket. He had whatever he had. The sun was going down, shadows become living things, a little kid rides a bike in a parking lot. It's cool, little kid, it's cool. Go on, get lost, go ride where you want.

LINCOLN BOULEVARD

I GREW UP HERE. I was little here. I watched Happy Days here. I played all kinds of games here. I watched *Giant Robot* when I lived here. It was so sad when Giant Robot flew into space with the evil one and blew up. Johnny Socko was crying. He lost his friend, the power to make his soul convictions real in the world. "No Giant Robot, No..."

Santa Monica, what happened? You got slick. You got therapy. You had surgery, a face lift, a standard of living lift. I don't know this place now. Don't you remember Johnny and Mark O'Brian? Their dad worked in the glass box at USA Gas. They didn't have any money, and he had drawers full of Penthouse. I couldn't believe it, naked women, and what about when I found those twenty joints on the steps? I gave them all to crazy Jerry, and I knew what they were, but not even that, Santa Monica, you were cool with your old people and your little kids: biddy basketball, Boy's Club craft shop, air hockey, playing baseball in the alley, a home run was anything hit into the old lady's yard, and 3 hour bike rides, crossing streets like crossing rivers of sangsara. Why don't you have a plaque to Mrs. Madison, beautiful old lady, lived across from Arby's and right behind my apartment. Her house was a two story, white painted clapboard, an island with a mechanic shop on one side and Len Sheridan Toyota on the other, right on Lincoln Blvd. She took me on tours of her house and showed me all the rooms and all the things that she collected, told me stories of where they came from. She had a piece of wood she found in the alley, all carved up by termites and on it she wrote, "By termite." She had these marbles that she boiled and the ribbon inside exploded and she had this funky jam made from a fruit tree in her yard. When she died they tore her house down as fast as they could and built a parking lot. There was an old man with a huge train set, smoking little locomotives speeding through the miniature tunnels and towns. The whole thing was two garages long.

My folks, I love them. They were just sad, filled with sadness that they did not create and could not get rid of, they got it from somewhere in their own damage, heart break, heart open, sad skin, sad light, there it is, the world is sad, things don't work, ghosts don't leave you alone, you don't always live for the things you ought to live for, you do things, mad things, hurtful things, and you don't know why you are doing them and it's not you, it's the sadness… but really, it is you, laying in bed, in the dark, listening to them crying, crashing into walls, and then the sounds of the world seep in between the leaves of the apartment tree behind your bedroom window, sirens, mostly as I remember, and traffic. Airplanes moving through stars shimmered like flying crowns. We listened to Mystery Radio while going to sleep, almost every night, and I remember, my mom telling me beautiful stories about the moon… Arby's Roast beef, Mobil Gas, Banner Carpets, drunk man on his ass.

Jack in the Box is still there, where me and my brother ate many times and got jumped, yes, by some older kids.

Fuck you, older kid jackers of Jack in the Box memory. I deny you and beat you and maim you in my perfect and vengeful mind, club you with an invention that I made up in my head because of you, a billy club with razor blades and knife blades that pop out, big long ones, and fire comes out the end and it kills you and all that are like you. You who would steal our money, who did, and denied us our Jumbo Jack. You have surely suffered at the hands of your own violence. It didn't matter, we went back to Jack in the Box anyway. There we sat and wrote notes with the bag man mute on Lincoln Blvd. He refused to talk, walked with papers stuffed into his ragged suit coat, white beard, shiny, lunatic wine eyes like a child, he wrote everything on pieces of paper taken from his pockets. We had full conversations with him this way. He ordered his coffee and pie from the counter girl this way. This was where I learned the meaning of words, I think, the old mute bum man, he wrote on scraps, on anything, to say what he needed to say. Words from strange pockets telling the world what you need. Little notes written on cards and advertisements for silver dollars and gold coins. The old man stank of wine and trash.

The genius muse angel serpent duende griot wino of light is naked on the bed of your body and soul, wanting you, in the butterfly position, in the screaming doves of milk position, in the raven with a dark night in its eye style, let's get with the skulls of mud, let's get naked, you and me, both of us, let's get womb deep, seed spilt, child holding, that's what it is, that is what we do… begin the world with each word we make, the coming of gems from a womb not seen, a love burned sun fusing a dream iris with the eye of the pigeon scuttling around the Arby's parking lot. It is no page of letters I have seen before, this, it is written on the flesh of the silence that surrounds us, here it is, hear it, chambered molecule of the universe. It sings eyes of flame and feathers of blood, a book of matches dropped by emptiness herself, surely it is the angel of death, it is annihilation, this is the end of the road, the lonesome long as memory road, this is it, this is the hand of the destroyer coming to you as you cross the street, count your change from the newspaper you just bought, counting you out and into the wounded moment of time where it all started from, here at Goddamn Jack in the Box, back in 1975.

But I don't die. I live forever in the divinity of this world's failures. Pep Boys, Library, Wallace Toys, spent my money on the Guns of Navrone... I am the keeper of the light bulbs. I smoke the knucklehead moon.

Life is a canvas, art. We make it, stretch it, we open it up and put it together, we spill all over it, it is ours to make what we will with it, but when is it good and when is it too much, when is it done, when we have done enough, and when must we find new surfaces, stretch ourselves again, and who is really doing the painting, who decides when to fuck and who to be with? Where do the dreams that burn us alive come from? Who made all of these toy soldiers? Who the stroke? Who the shade determines? Dost thou know the hand that moves thine? No way, no one knows. You live like you do, yourself, making all the decisions, act like you know which way to go, know how far the street turns, but of course that isn't the case. No one knows who is driving this thing, who is gonna get on and turn your life upside the down street, who is gonna get on and have your baby, make your eye into eyes, no one knows who is gonna open your heart and bring you out of yourself, no one knows anything, and if you do, well, that's a different story.

Oh, old beatnik ghost, who are you there on the 3rd street bus stop, making your transfer to Heaven, of course, walking the ghostly trees, combing the sand for Buffalo nickels and holy radio juice? Your skin lectured by the sun, finger to lips, bohemian beach riff-raff, your shacks and sea castles are gone. Honest John's Hot Dogs, Bavarian Wrestlers, A child Named Rainbow, gone. But I saw you playing chess when I was young, and I heard you. You were drunk and mad, sparring with Groucho and losing all for poetry. Insane. Your music plays loud out the window of my soul.

The Third Street Promenade mall, a very successful and popular mall, money in the walls here. You can feel it. Everything looks new, right, not a speck of decay, full of colorful shoppers, good people, no bad habits, it has all been taken care of. I love the mall. You want something, you buy it. You get hungry, you eat. I shop, I eat burgers, I don't live in a log cabin, I am in this world, I need my car, I watch lots of television, I get mad during sporting events, I think illegal thoughts, and here we are at the mall, the new mall, and the old mall, it was new too, once, everything moving to new, and it is full of people, good, they are the only ones we stand a chance of talking to, and look at them, God love them, pretending that they like this stuff, pretending that there is something to look for, something to be interested in, something that they need?

Sure, they need. We all need, and that is all there is to it. That is what I am saying, we have always needed, we should be called "Needans" instead of humans. Man, what is that short for? Maniacs? We need the same thing that we needed when we jumped out of the tree, we need the same thing that the guy with the paint in the cave needed, the same thing that the slave at the top of the pyramid needed... the mall is full with our terrestrial bound need to believe... anything. Looka the mall: lotsa colors, Wolfgang Puck, the soft porn of middle class want, it's all there.

It is all about light, being moths trapped in light... about light, what is the light? Waves, pieces, scraps and shrapnel of the sun which we live off of, which we define ourselves by, which have been taken and shaped with shadows into moving images of ourselves, and every self-respecting location of civilized human community has a movie theatre, covering the deep need to fuck till we drop, everyone at the mall really longs to tear the walls down and fuck in the flames, fuck whoever you want, random fucking, fuck some guys, fuck a dog, fuck the wall, fuck the plant, get down with a coupla gals, a coupla more boys, get nasty, get rooster, get animal, go for the kiddies, go for the tying it up, use a knife, bully your companion with a club, shove a something up the butt of someone, it's free, but there are movies and no one needs to fuck anyone, which is good, who would be able to handle that kind of stress on the emotional fabric of our basic social unit of monogamy? The government would have to invent a sexual plague to instill the fear of God in the sexual rebels, which of course already happened.

Really everyone here wants the burger, I want the burger, I love the burger, 'cause I am hungry, the prophetic burger, the food of future thought, gimme a Goddamn Double Cheese, rockets to the stars, I think of space travel at the mall, why? What do we think we are going to find out there? What if there is something else, someone else? Why do we need to know them, why do we need to communicate? We can't even do it down here, with ourselves. I don't care. I just wanna get my car.

Believe it or not, I liked the old mall better. I liked its mess of decaying theatres and mossy wishing wells, and lonely drunkard bars, the winos that slept there at night, the dime stores and toy stores, Europa the huge yardage store, the eternal flame for the soldiers up at Wilshire, Wallace Toys. There was a bakery with old ladies working the counter, and cakes hung up on the wall so you could see what designs they offered. There was a hot dog restaurant right on the street where sunburned unlovely people would wait for the bus and get a dog and a drink, and be drunk after a day at the beach. There were a lot more drunk people around in the Seventies. I remember that because I remember the breasts of this woman were hanging out of her top, her titty skin was so pale against the burned, she was having a drink and talking to a man, waiting for the bus back into Los Angeles. She wore sun glasses, there was sand on the sidewalk, cigarette smoke in the air, and someone drank a beer.

The mall was wonderful for its desolate days at dimestores, a haven for retired folk, there was a JJ Newberry's. These people here, they don't need a JJ Newberry, they are doing well, they do not befriend the pigeon as the last human contact of their life, they are well off and they got the right thing on their mind, they got the money to pay for parking, they are having a good time, Starbuck's Coffee is right there, and sitting there, within this, right in front of Starbucks are the punk runaways, spider haired, drug addict, loser freak kids, just like there always has been and will be and is at every suburban shopping culture palace, the flowers of nowhere, sitting in a world where no one has anything to live for except the ability to participate in the commerce of the mall, nothing greater and nothing more mysterious than our own creations, our own knowledge, our own images, our own nature, the young live to die, because alive don't look like much on these channels of Angelic nightmare, we are fed, but not well, what about the need, what about our lovely wound? We give it up so easily, assign it a program, an addiction, a fashion and call it done, healed, no questions please, wanting only the soft deception of answer, tell me what is so, answer this ringing, answer this phone, the bell, be there, answer.

Make me a cop. Kill all that would dream, kill myself and all that might be beautiful in me, kill it with mall processed air, kill it with the prescriptions of fantasy exhibited by the doctors of imagination, kill it with the false rhythms of freedom that are pumped out of dropped Honda gangster cars, kill it with the false dollars of empty wealth, kill it with the shallow extremity of our rock and roll, drug addled, porn saturated mind, kill it by making it live, kill it by caring, kill it with parents who don't care and teachers who don't know, and lovers who don't love, kill it with race, my race, your race, all the races, the white race, the black race, the brown race, the yellow, kill it with your hating Christs and jealous gods.

No one can be anything but what they are, and nothing that we are shall be denied, be this ground and this time and be your past, your line, be your fathers, your mothers, but be always the miracle. Destroy all the lies that divide, divide you from yourself, that keep you from the sea. We are not just this skin, or just this life or these possessions, no matter how history and money have made us, as different as music and cooking may be, when it comes down to the belly, the bone and the sky, we all have the same shadowed scar in our hands trying to bear the light that is without end, without answer.

We are all hurt, everyone on this bus on this street, in these houses, behind the curtains, in the kitchen, in the closet, in the toilet, in the light, hurt and pin cushioned, everyone, been left, molested, murdered, abandoned, starved, buried, forgotten, beaten, made stupid to the world, harmed, victimized, denied, lived a lie, been lied to, the last to know, the only one to care, everyone on this bus has been done to and have done it all ourselves, and here we go anyway, go to work, go to hell, go to get the car, got to get drunk, got to get the worm, to continue the misery, to take it somewhere else, to stop it, altogether, but how does it stop, how does it end? There's no end, it is what makes us alive, heart all over the floor, gut strings in every hand full of sunshine that you breathe. Are you gonna deny all the vicious angelic flaming coffins of love that cause you pain, that give you joy, that destroy you, that make you? You weep at the smell of chestnuts, you die in the midst of a song you don't even know the name of. It is nutty, wacko, no one gets it, but you, you thought you had love, then you don't and you are sad. You must be or it wasn't love, and you won't have love again, bright and shiny daggers of love, vicious love, bitter love, wonderful love that makes me hate things, love that is holy and battered like the streets, going in all the directions of day and night.

Oh, hallelujah, Samson, ours is hard ass love. The sun keeps us happening like a blessing or curse, both, I suppose. What do you pray for, city of both hands, city of angels, city of poverty, city of glamourless glamour, city of hunger, city of bones, city of hamburger, city of politicians with no jobs, city of movie stars and no galaxy, city of roses and weeds, city of city, city of dog, city of machine street cat feet, of the peasant mind, of the dark sky lit purple, orange, that cries, city without, of the without, with no history, history not seen but inside us, city of smokestack illusion, freeway stars of the black and white and brown, the vacant crowd, the silent loud, the deathful proud, the loveless fools, and the yellow, the purple, the butter, the better, the net of nets and light of lights, the continental ending post of donut shows and pornographic rows of yellow hotels, city of killers, city of smoke of steel glass eyes locked in an idiot television gaze, city of fuck me or fight me but please give me something.

City of love on quiet streets, in backyards beneath bougainvillaea morning glory, shhhh, baby talking in her sleep, city of naked hatred hated time, sun, sun burning holes into your neck, spray can flame the heart of fame, gimme justice, gimme my peace, hate the hating, city of pigs on a leash, of wild machines not eating what they eat, city of many people but no kind, of many races but no one, city of memory, for whom? City of dreams, but no sleep, city of the sea, angels in the waves, really, I've seen them, it was late, no one was awake.

This city, a woman, woman ground with sunsets like visions. Spider whispered cloud tongues speaking feather eyes of cumulus columns of windy moans held still and lusty cold above us all, seen thousands of them, and think with them dropping in my hands, this is the end of the continent, think this, say it, until the fact so obvious becomes a tongue in my bones, becomes flesh and slips in through me. There is a language for all of this. There is a meter for the reasons. I know it.

City with no sides, spread like a carpet of moths from the hills to the steel sea, city with no no, all comes to you, through you and finally from you, and none will admit it. None see you. All they see is a red carpet to nowhere. But I invoke you and create you and when I die they can say he rode these busses, drove these cars, walked these streets, made his family and love here, he lived here, he was these people.

I am the lost old man looking over the bluff into the sea. I am the woman with five kids selling hot dogs in front of the night club. I am the Chinese grandmother letting her kid pee on the street. I am sorry. I had to do it, the kid was gonna wet his pants. I am not being high minded and holy. I am full-minded. I am full- blooded human bean dip, ugly shit, the smell and piss. No offense to anyone, but I am all of you and it is uncomfortable, I can't hold it in!

SECOND STREET

THE WHOLE CITY, THE WHOLE ride, coming down to this block, all the subterranean flowers of flame, malignant ovum, the blessing trains, all the world of tires and tired souls, the streets that strung out streets to all the streets that ever got dreamed or beaten, bled or blossomed, imagined only, real forever, gone before the end of the next page of rain, streets falling in robes of bones and blood, clothes made of hands and mouths, like a fit of rainy love. It all comes down to here and the next pay-phone I find.

Walk to the bluff, look out over the sea: the lights are teeth, a glittering dog, the phantoms of smog. Waves, one after the other, speaking about a darker thing beneath, come up and fall apart and get sucked back into the night. The waves fall the same as they have forever. Let that be a lesson to you, young man.

This, right here, is the end of the road, this is the end of the continent, that is the Pacific Ocean. There should be some kind of plaque or display. What would it have? Golden slave ships filled with the pieces of the White House, a picture of a freeway, a record, Guadalupe walking Juan Diego across a border that isn't there, the first can of dog food, some pornographic titties, a big gun, a television stuffed into a brain, Jesus on a flaming locomotive chasing hot love west, a tight buttocks of undecided gender... There is no sign though, just the ocean, which is enough. Great water of creation. God is out there, drifting in a drunkard's boat, mumbling to himself, too far from any land to know which way to go.

The ocean holds all that has passed in its salt. Oh, humans of now and time to come, all we have is each other, my girls, mother, father. All we have is each other. All we have is each other.

Good night, bones.
  Good night, dogs.
  Good night, pumpkin fields.
  Good night, car head lights.
  Good night, Flying Saucer.
  Good night, perpetual airplanes of song.
  Good night, Thomas Jefferson.
  Good night, Paris, Africa.
  Good night, Jerusalem.
  Good night, Mexico.
  Good night, Magic Mountain.
One day you all will be forgotten, but for now, we are alive. That is all I know.

"Hari! It's me, Abee."
  "Good. Your car is done."

STEVE ABEE was born and raised in Santa Monica, California. He began writing after high school when he held a job as an orderly at St. John's Hospital. His mind started to unfold itself and he thought if he was going to save it he better start writing things down. After dropping out of UC Santa Cruz where he studied with Lucille Clifton, he returned to Los Angeles and worked as a cook, a furniture mover and a taxi driver. He graduated from UCLA and has been teaching English to seventh graders in Silverlake since 1995. Abee has performed his work at all manner of performance spaces up and down the West Coast. His work has appeared in a variety of zines, chapbooks and literary magazines. His other titles include *Jerusalem Donuts*, a spoken word CD, and *King Planet*, a collection of short stories and poems. Abee resides with his wife, Cathy, and their daughters, Penelope and Maya, in Echo Park, Los Angeles.

Jesse Hopkins

OTHER TITLES FROM PHONY LID

UNBORN AGAIN • S.A. GRIFFIN

A new collection of undeniable, mind-blowing LA poetry from the award-winning writer, original Carma Bum and co-editor of *The Outlaw Bible of American Poetry*. The world according to S.A. Griffin: "First, he's dealing you savvy urban pathos from the bottom of a beer-stained deck. Then he's beefing it up with homages to that Chinaski dude. Then he's steeping you in the raunchiest need you'll ever want to ponder, or tickling your innards so hard you're wet with laughter. Moments seize you like the eyes of a desperate dreamer." —*Wanda Coleman*

128 pages, 5x7, with a full color cover by Louis Metz.

ISBN: 1-930935-17-X $12.00 US postpaid

ERRATIC SLEEP IN A COLD HOTEL • MARIE KAZALIA

"Evocative, powerful narrative poems take the reader through pockets of intriguing urban ecology, poverty hotels and near third-world conditions for a revealing look at the cheap hustles of drug addicts, dejects, schizoids and unfortunates. Her acute observations are tempered with an understated humor to all the more poignantly engage the reader in a woman's struggle with substandard conditions in American life, where her courage is evident in every poem." —*Koon Woon*

80 pages, 5x7, b&w cover photograph by Cesar Rubio.

ISBN: 1-930935-15-3 $11.00 US postpaid

DILLINGER'S THOMPSON • TODD MOORE

"This next entry in Todd Moore's epic materwork in progress, **Dillinger**, *Dillinger's Thompson* is an erotic journey into the American psyche masterfully acheived in verse via the voice of Dillinger's machine gun speaking in the person of the criminal icon's phallus. Exceptional, unforgettable and compelling work from one of the truly great poets of our time." —*S.A. Griffin*

Also includes "Machine Gun Dreams," an introduction to the Dillinger epic by the Todd Moore, reviews and publication history of **Dillinger**.

56 pages, 4x7, b&w collage by Danger.

ISBN: 1-930935-25-0 $7.00 US postpaid

WRITE FOR A FREE CATALOGUE of these and other available titles in fiction, poetry, art and comics.

PHONY LID BOOKS
PoBox 29066 • Los Angeles, Ca 90029
www.phonylid.com

THE NEW LITERATURE IS INDEPENDENT